KILLING GROUND . . .

"Ride!" Ki thundered. They galloped ahead through the open woods, then veered to the left for more tree protection as a shot came too close.

In the trees, Ki slid off his mount. "Don't get too near him," he said and rushed forward, using the trees for cover. Jessie turned sharply. Now she could get behind the robber. She rode hard through the trees, then circled around the spot where she figured the shooter must be lying.

Jessie filled the magazine on her repeater, tied her mount, and slid off. She moved slowly, pausing beside a two-foot pine.

No sound. No movement ahead.

Then a man stepped from behind a tree. She lifted the rifle and aimed at his chest.

"Hold it right there. The game is over," Jessie told him. "Your killing days are ~~over~~

*   *   *

SPECIAL PR

Turn to the back of this book for an exciting excerpt from the magnificent new series . . .

RAILS WEST!

. . . the grand and epic story of the West's first railroads—and the brave men and women who forged an American dream.

—◆— WESLEY ELLIS —◆—

LONE STAR

AND THE
SAN DIEGO BONANZA

J

JOVE BOOKS, NEW YORK

LONE STAR AND THE SAN DIEGO BONANZA

A Jove Book / published by arrangement with
the author

PRINTING HISTORY
Jove edition / May 1993

ISBN: 0-515-11104-X

Jove Books are published by The Berkley Publishing Group,
200 Madison Avenue, New York, New York 10016.
The name "JOVE" and the "J" logo
are trademarks belonging to Jove Publications, Inc.

PRINTED IN THE UNITED STATES OF AMERICA

10 9 8 7 6 5 4 3 2 1

★

Chapter 1

Jessica Starbuck and Ki stepped down from the big Concord stagecoach with the Wells Fargo lettering on the side and looked for her luggage. The two of them had just arrived in the little mining town of Julian, some sixty miles north and east of San Diego, California.

Three short and squarely built young men lounged in front of the Julian Hotel and watched with obvious delight as the fall wind whipped Jessica's traveling skirt up, revealing a trim ankle. The three wore rough miner's clothes and had the features of Cornish men. They seemed to be just out of the tunnels and looking for some fun.

One rushed up to Jessica, caught her shoulders, and waltzed her around the boardwalk. Ki was pulling luggage from the top of the coach and didn't see what happened.

Jessica glared at the young Cornishman, her green eyes snapping. She gripped her hands together at her waist and jolted them upward, smashing the young man's arms aside and his hands off her. She jumped back, her shoulder-length coppery blond hair swirling around her cameo face.

"No!" she shouted.

Ki spun around, one hand reaching in a pocket and coming out with a deadly *shuriken,* the eight-pointed and -bladed

1

throwing star. At once he saw the two other men advancing on them. Jessie's hand darted into her reticule and came out with her favorite .38 Colt revolver, mated to a .44 Colt frame.

"No," she said again, her frown adding emphasis.

The three Cornishmen chuckled.

"Lass, we're supposed to be afeared of the likes of you and your Chinaman go-fetch-man?" the broadest of the three snorted.

Jessica fired a round into the planks by his feet where he stood three yards away, and he laughed harder, striding toward her. She shot him in the right thigh, and he bellowed in pain, limping to one side. The one who had waltzed with her came up with a weapon of his own, a small derringer in his left hand.

Ki's hand snapped forward, and the eight-pointed star blade spun toward the miner. Two of the *shuriken* blades sunk deeply into the Cornishman's left wrist, which immediately spurted blood. The jolt smashed the small pistol from his hand.

The miner screamed in pain, looked down at the star in amazement, tore it free from his flesh, and dropped it. He grabbed his wrist with his right hand to slow the bleeding.

All three of the Cornishmen turned and bolted down the street beside the hotel and up the hill away from the stage.

The driver on top of the Concord tossed Ki a leather traveling case. "About time them three got some comeuppance. They been bothering my incoming passengers for two weeks now." The driver, a tall, thin man in his forties, wiped sweat off his forehead with a pale blue-shirted arm. "Reckon they won't be messing around here again for a few days."

Two men coming down the hotel steps when the incident started had hurried back inside when they heard gunfire. Now they looked out, saw no danger and came down the steps. They went the other way along the street.

"Will your sheriff want a report about this?" Jessie asked the driver.

"Sheriff? He'd be down in San Diego. Big county here. We got a town marshal, but he's a no-good far as the law goes. Doubt if two gunshots would even get him out of his game

2

of checkers down at the city building." He tossed down two more satchels and a carpetbag.

"I was accosted on Main Street, and a man was just shot here," Jessie said, frowning as she looked at the driver. "Doesn't the lawman here in Julian care about something like this?"

The driver stepped down, from the high seat to the boardwalk. He shook his head, his face serious as he considered what Jessie had said. "Nope, he don't. That's about the size of it, miss. Our town marshal ain't concerned about lawbreakers. Which means we ain't got much law and order here in Julian. Mostly we take care of things ourselves, if'n something needs doing. Like you did with them three no-good jackass miners."

Ki lifted his black brows slightly at the statement, then picked up their three bags and waited for Jessie. She watched the Wells Fargo man a moment more, then turned and marched along the boardwalk and up the steps to the hotel.

Jessie attracted attention wherever she went. She was tall, lissome, and in her late twenties, with firm, full breasts, sensuously rounded thighs, and tight, high buttocks that her green tweed riding jacket and skirt couldn't conceal. She wore a silk blouse, low-heeled boots, and a brown Stetson with a thong under her chin. Her pretty face held a pert nose, and most could find a trace of feline audacity in her widely set eyes. A dimpled chin, and sometimes a shrewd and humorous twist to her lips, completed the picture.

Ki, her protector and companion, followed her into the hotel. Ki was half-American and half-Japanese, wore his black hair shoulder length, and was clean shaven except for a pencil-thin mustache. His almond shaped eyes gave away his ancestry. Ki had thin lips, and his skin was bronzed by the sun.

Today he wore a lightweight blue-gray traveling suit, sky-blue shirt, and a shoestring tie. His Stetson was flat-crowned, and on his feet were black, ankle-high Wellington boots. A braided black leather band wrapped around his forehead.

They registered at the Julian Hotel and took rooms side by side on the second floor. Five minutes later Jessie had unpacked her clothes into the small dresser and was ready for business. She knocked on Ki's door with the telegram in her hand.

3

The wire had come to the Starbuck Ranch in western Texas only four days before. She read it again:

"JESSIE STARBUCK, STARBUCK RANCH, WESTERN TEXAS. YOUR FRIEND, LAWSON BLAINE, MURDERED HERE A WEEK AGO. URGENTLY REQUEST YOUR HELP TO SOLVE HIS KILLING. HIS DEATH LISTED HERE AS AN ACCIDENT. IT CANNOT BE. HE SPOKE OF YOU OFTEN. I'M PLEADING FOR YOUR HELP. PLEASE COME IF YOU CAN. MRS. LAWSON (AGATHA) BLAINE. JULIAN, CALIFORNIA."

The wire spun Jessie back five years before, when Lawson Blaine had been a top hand on the Starbuck ranch. He had been with them for six years and had become the second most valuable hand, next to the foreman. And he'd known there was little chance that Ed Wright would quit or retire as foreman of the Circle Star spread.

Jessie had been more than a little in love with Lawson that last summer, and she tried to talk him into staying. He said he had to move on. He had no right to claim her, and he certainly couldn't outpoint Ed Wright for the foreman's job. It had been a loving and a tearful good-bye. He had written once from Wyoming, and after that she had lost track of him. Lawson said he wasn't much on writing letters.

Now she was in Julian to set right a terrible wrong and to find who killed Lawson and see that he was punished properly. There was no possibility that she could stay away once she knew that Lawson Blaine had been killed.

Ki came to the door. He had changed into his working clothes. He wore tight-fitting denim jeans, a light blue pullover twill cotton shirt with no collar and a well-worn brown leather vest with several pockets. On his feet were brown sandals the color of his tanned legs.

"We're a week late on this killing, Ki. I'll find the widow; you talk with the town marshal and the undertaker and see what you can learn about the death."

Five minutes later Jessie had asked at the Julian General Store on Main Street how she might find Mrs. Agatha Blaine.

4

The postmistress in the store told her to go down two blocks and up B Street two blocks to a small white house with a picket fence and lots of flowers around it.

The walkway from the dirt street up to the door was lined with rose bushes, carefully trimmed and still blooming. Against the front of the house on both sides of the door stood lilac bushes with a few late blooms of deep purple flowers.

Jessie went up the walk and knocked on the door. It opened at once.

A thin, pretty woman in her early twenties stood there in a calico housedress. Her hair was a dark jumble around her shoulders. Her eyes were dark, and black shadows showed under them. A flash of recognition lit her sad eyes.

"You must be Miss Jessica Starbuck. Won't you please come in."

"I am. You're Agatha?"

The woman nodded and held the door wider, and Jessie walked into the clean front room. It was sparsely furnished but done with good taste. Everything was ready for an Army general's inspection.

"I'm so glad you came!" Agatha burst out. Tears flooded her eyes, and Jessie caught her arm and led her to a sofa, where they both sat. Agatha tried to stop the tears, but they came again. She leaned on Jessie's shoulder, and a few moments later sat up and wiped away the moisture.

"I'm sorry. I can't believe that he's gone. I hear a noise and look up and smile because I expect Lawson to stride through the door the way he always did. . . ."

She closed her eyes and slowly shook her head. "I know all of this grief is unnatural. I should be over it by now. You see, he's the first person I truly loved who I ever lost."

Jessie hugged the woman, patted her back, and talked gently and soothingly.

"Agatha, I know a little of how you feel. He was my good friend for six years, and toward the end I was in love with him myself, but it couldn't be." She eased away and watched Agatha. "Now the official mourning time is over. Now we set out to find who killed Lawson and bring them to justice. Can you help me?

Agatha wiped her eyes again and slowly nodded. "Yes. I must be strong now. I can do anything you need done."

"Good. First, what was Lawson excited about the last few days? What was he talking about? Did he have any big plans or was he working on something with someone else?"

Agatha twisted her long dark hair around her finger and then undid it, only to twist it again as she frowned and thought back. "No big plans. He said he hoped to work up to be foreman of the day shift and then eventually assistant manager at the Ready Relief mine."

"Did he talk about the owners? Who are they?"

"Oh, he said he got along fine with the owner, Judge Washington Maxwell. He got three promotions and was leader of one section."

"What did he do at the mine?"

"He had a good job. He worked in the final step of the process, where the gold amalgam from the stamping mill is heated and refined and poured into the molds to make the gold bars."

"A responsible job?"

Agatha's eyes lit up. "Oh, it sure was. One mistake here and the work of a hundred men could be lost in a few seconds."

Jessie cocked her head to one side and listened. "What's that continuous noise, Agatha?"

"What noise?" She laughed. "Oh, I don't even hear it anymore. That's the stamp mill about a quarter of a mile up the hill, at the Eagle mine. It runs twenty-four hours a day."

"It's been a time since I've been to a mine. I'll have to look it over. Your husband worked at the Ready Relief mine, you said. How far is that from here?"

"Maybe five miles. We have a horse that Lawson rode back and forth."

Jessie reached out and put her hand over Agatha's. "I'm going to ask you some questions that might seem cruel, but I need to know. Do you understand?"

Agatha frowned but nodded.

"If you don't want to answer some of them, just tell me so. Now, did Lawson do much gambling in the saloons?"

"He did some before we were married. We've been married two years now . . . would have been next week." Tears threatened to come again.

"When he gambled, was it for lots of money?"

"He told me he never lost more than five dollars at a time gambling. Once he won fifty, but he lost it back the next few nights. He didn't even go to the saloons after we were married. He said he had everything he wanted right here at home."

Jessica looked around the living room. "I'd guess you don't have any children."

Agatha shook her head. "We wanted to. Just didn't seem like it happened. Must have been my fault."

"Now, Agatha, think hard on this. Were there any kind of organizations or groups around this area he was a member of? Was there a vigilante committee?"

"Oh, no. Nothing like that. The sheriff from San Diego even gets mad when we hold a miner's court. We tell him if he'd come up here or at least post a deputy sheriff up here, we wouldn't have to go to miner court justice. San Diego is a huge county, almost two hundred miles wide in spots."

"He didn't belong to a union or a group of workers, or anything like that?" Jessie asked.

"Oh, gracious no. He said he'd heard of some labor unions back east, but none out here. Lawson used to read *The New York Times*. They sent one copy a week to him by mail, and it arrived about two weeks after it was published, but he loved it."

Jessie felt she was stumbling around in a dark mine tunnel and not making any progress.

"Did Lawson have any enemies, anyone angry enough at him to deliberately kill him?"

Agatha's eyes went wide, and she leaned back in surprise. "Oh, no. Everyone I knew liked Lawson. He was a friend to anyone who wanted to be friendly. He was probably the best-liked man in the whole Ready Relief mine."

"Then why did someone kill him?"

Tears came again. Agatha slashed them away angrily this time. "I don't know. I've asked myself that same question a thousand times, and I never can find an answer."

Jessie stood. Nothing. She had nothing to go on. She held out her hand, but Agatha put out her arms, and the two women hugged.

"I'm so glad you came, Jessie. I've been angry because I know Lawson's death wasn't an accident. Here in town, nobody will listen to me."

"Someone will start to listen now," Jessie said. "You can count on it. I'll be back to talk to you soon." Jessie hurried out the door and down the block, toward the small cafe on Main street where she and Ki had arranged to meet.

Ki stared at the small man with the pot belly, bald head, and wide suspenders holding up his britches. He wore no shirt; only his fire-red long johns showed under the braces. Myles Zane looked up from the checkerboard set on an empty nail keg and scowled back at his visitor.

"Young man, I'm in the middle of a ten-cent checker game here, if you don't mind. I can't afford to lose another game to this skinflint here, and I don't mind telling you he's two pieces ahead of me right now. What in tarnation did you ask me?"

Ki had long ago learned the art of controlling his emotions, and now he quietly repeated his question.

"I asked you if you have a file or any records on the sudden death of Lawson Blaine, a worker at the Ready Relief mine."

"Oh, couple of weeks ago. I remember that one. Nope, not a thing. That's outside of my jurisdiction."

"Just what is your jurisdiction, Marshal? As town marshal you cover what territory? This town isn't incorporated, so there are no definite limits as to what's in town and out of town. Wouldn't you say so?"

"Reckon you're about right, son. Now, if you don't mind, I intend to beat this cross-minded maverick of a whistle-toed tomcat here, and I don't need no more distraction from you. Chances are the death certificate has been signed by old Doc Raleigh. Don't know for sure. Might check with the county recorder in San Diego. Seems to me that death certificates go down there now."

The marshal turned his back on Ki and pondered his next move on the checkerboard.

Ki stood there a moment, then turned and walked out of the small office. His face didn't reveal any emotion. He was more curious than angry. Why did a town of this size hire a marshal who seemingly did nothing about upholding the law?

His next stop was the undertaker's, a building on B Street half a block up the hill from Main. Most of Julian was built on a small snarl of hills and dips and swales. From Main Street moving north the lettered streets climbed uphill for two blocks, then stopped.

Ki found the place, Julian Undertakers, and tried the door. It was not locked. Inside he caught the sharp smell of chemicals and wasn't sure what they were. The room he entered was a lobby about ten feet deep. A desk sat there and two chairs.

As soon as he closed the door, a man came through a curtain covering a door at the far side of the room. He was dressed all in black and had just slipped into his suit jacket but had not yet folded down the collar around his neck. He was of medium height, had a somber expression, and Ki felt at once his antagonism.

"We don't usual do Chinaman funerals," the man said.

"Fine with me, I'm not Chinese. What I'm interested in is the death about two weeks ago of Lawson Blaine. What can you tell me about how he was killed and the condition of the body when you picked it up?"

"Oh, sorry, I just figured . . . Well, this gent you mention was brought to me. Happens lots of times. The mine owner said the man was caught between two loaded ore carts. Those little carts weigh about two tons when filled with ore or that worthless schist rock. This gent was badly done in. His chest and back were smashed up and flattened together."

"His head was not damaged?"

"Fact is not a scratch on it. Just his chest and back."

"Could the man have been shot, then smashed up that way? Was there much bleeding around the smashed area?"

"No bleeding. Come to think of it there should have been some, unless of course his heart was stopped before he was crushed." The undertaker lifted his brows. "Uh-oh. You must be coming here looking for something to stir up a ruckus. They said it was an accident out at the mill when they brought

9

him in." Myles scowled and shook his head. "If there was a bullet or two in that man's chest or back, I didn't find them. Course, I didn't look, 'cause I didn't think I needed to."

"Could two slugs have been there?" Ki pressed.

"Oh, damn yes, easy could have been there. He was mashed up until he wasn't more than four inches thick, like you hit a potato on a rock with a cousin Jack eight-pound hammer."

"Who signed the death certificate?"

"Not me, not qualified. Old Doc Raleigh did the honors. He even come down and looked at the body. Usual he don't do that. He's having trouble getting around now."

"Where is Lawson buried? We could get a court order to dig him up."

"He ain't buried. His wife said he always told her if he was ever dead, he wanted to be cremated. We ain't got no fancy equipment here, so she decided on a pyre, like they do in India. We had a right nice ceremony. Most of the townsfolk turned out. Regular funeral and all, then the widow lady was supposed to light the fire, but she couldn't, so they made me do it. Took near six hours to burn it all up."

"Which means there's no body to look at for bullets," Ki said softly. He thanked the undertaker. There didn't seem any sense in bothering the old doctor. He waved at the undertaker and walked downhill toward Main Street.

Ki had just turned around the corner near the Julian Hotel, onto Main, when a rifle shot snarled and at the same time he felt hot lead slice through the air what seemed like only a few inches from his head.

★

Chapter 2

Ki dove behind a freight wagon that stood next to the boardwalk and tried to locate from where the shot had come. He checked for the usual telltale white smoke of the black powder, but couldn't find any. The shot had come from across the street.

Ki peeked over the top of the wagon from a different spot but could find no smoke. Then he caught movement behind the low false front of the barbershop across the street, and he ducked.

A fraction of a second later a lead slug bored into the side of the wagon, a foot from his shoulder. It splintered the wood and passed on through.

Ki never carried a gun. And this was too far a throw for his blades. Another shot slammed into the wagon box, but this one didn't go through. Ki saw a team and wagon coming down the street. He waited until they were directly between him and the gunman, then sprinted in a zigzag course to the side of the wagon. Two shots slashed through the dust and dirt at his feet, but both missed. He reached the side of the wagon as it rolled along the street and crouched behind the rig for fifty feet, then sprinted to the storefronts on the far side of the street, where the gunman had been. He stepped into a real estate office, nodded to the people, and asked if there was a back door. A man in a stiff collar and

11

white shirt pointed to a door in the rear, and Ki hurried through it.

Ki wasn't running, but he covered the space quickly, like a stalking cougar or panther. He darted out the back door of the office and looked to his right, where he saw a small barber pole marking the back door of the trim palace. A man hurried down from the roof on a wooden ladder nailed to the back of the building.

Ki ran thirty feet, then threw one of the *shuriken* blades. It sliced through the climber's right ankle, neatly severing his Achilles tendon. The man screamed, dropped his rifle, and fell the last four feet to the ground. He hit hard, groaned, and rolled over, pawing for the six-gun on his hip.

Ki kicked the weapon out of his hand just as he drew it from leather.

"You won't need that," Ki said. He picked up the fallen rifle and smelled the barrel. It had been fired only minutes ago. "Why?" Ki asked.

"What the hell you talking about, Chinaman?"

"I'm Japanese, not Chinese. Why did you try to kill me just now when I was in the street?"

"Not me. I was up there fixing the roof."

"With a rifle?"

A man came out the back of the barbershop. He had a comb behind his ear and held a shaving mug and brush.

"Who the hell just ran across my roof?"

Ki pointed to the man on the ground.

"Guess you got him. I don't hold with nobody using my roof as a shooting gallery. Sure, I heard the shots. At least four of them, rifle shots. Think I'm deaf?" The barber shrugged. "Guess you got him. No more affair of mine." He turned and walked back into the barbershop.

Ki drew his *tanto* from the lacquered sheath thrust into the waistband of his jeans. The short, curved knife was kept scalpel-sharp. He pushed it flat against the downed man's throat.

The bushwhacker on the ground was in his twenties, bearded. His hat had fallen off in the scramble and showed long dark hair. He had eyebrows that grew together over his nose, and his eyes were dark and angry.

"What the hell's with the blade? You already cut my leg. I want a doctor."

"You haven't answered my question, and at times I lose my patience with trash like you."

"Easy, Japo, easy. No sense I get hurt anymore. I shot at you 'cause a guy gave me twenty dollars. That's a month's wages around these parts, case you're a stranger. Now, help me get to the doc."

"Who gave you the money?"

"Can't say."

Ki moved the blade and drew a thin two-inch line across the man's chin. It was deep enough to seep out blood, and a moment later the line was red and the wounded man's eyes went wide. He screeched in pain.

"Whenever a man tries to kill someone, the target is legally permitted to defend himself and kill his attacker. Is this not true here? Self-defense?"

"Yeah, sure, but . . ."

"Who gave you the money?"

The man on the ground swallowed hard, looked at Ki and then at the curved blade an inch from his nose. "Yeah, all right. Guess I can tell you. I'm getting out of town anyway. What do I care? His name was Kerr, Burl Kerr. Met him in the saloon. He's been around town a long time. Not sure what he does. Always seems to have money. Now can I go see the doctor?"

"Why did he say he wanted me dead?"

"Didn't say. For twenty bucks he didn't have to say."

Ki stood. "I should kill you and leave you here for the buzzards. This time you get away easy. Don't try it again, or you'll die a little at a time for two long painful hours. Now, get out of here. You won't be able to walk. Get the doctor to stitch that tendon back together." Ki turned and walked away quickly without a backward glance. He had judged that the man didn't have a hideout; nothing showed in any of the usual places.

Jessie stood in front of the Bonanza Cafe tapping one toe on the boardwalk. She looked down the street, saw Ki, and moved to meet him.

"Trouble?"

13

He told her about the sniper and the name of Burl Kerr.

"What we need is a person in town we can trust," Jessica said. "Besides Agatha Blaine. I doubt if she knows much more about the town than Lawson told her. A homebody."

"Let's try the cafe," Ki said. They went in, found an empty booth near the counter, and sat down. The waitress eyed Ki as soon as they came in. She was attractive, short, dark-haired, and a little heavy, with large breasts. Her white blouse had two buttons open at the top, and a bead of sweat rolled down from her chin, heading for the cleavage between her breasts.

Ki made a point of watching it, then looked up at her and grinned.

"What's good today?" he asked.

The girl smiled. "I am, but we also have vegetable soup and sandwiches that ain't too bad."

Ki had almost opened his mouth when Jessie swept in. "I'll have the soup and a cheese sandwich."

Ki ordered the same and coffee. When the waitress left, Ki nodded. "I think we just found our honest source of information for Julian. Waitresses hear a lot more than most of us think they do."

After they had eaten, Jessie left to rent a pair of saddle horses from the Julian livery, two blocks over. "Give it a try," Jessica said softly as she left the booth.

The waitress came back to clear their things, and when the booth was clean, she returned and sat down across from Ki. "Was she your wife, lover, or friend?"

"You're direct, aren't you?" He held out his hand. "She is my good friend and my employer. I'm Ki. What's your name?"

"Everyone calls me Happy. I'm Happy Tucker." She moved her shoulders so her her breasts jiggled. "Ki. What an interesting name. You're new in town, aren't you?"

"Yes, and I need your help. I'm trying to find out who killed a man a couple of weeks ago. I need someone I can trust who knows the town."

"Is the pay good?"

"Not that good. I'd want you to stay working here and keep your ears open."

14

he eased away from her so they both could sit on the side of the bunk.

"That was good," Ki said

"Better than that. It was the best I've ever had." She leaned in and kissed his lips. "I've never been loved by a Japanese man before. You were just fantastic!"

As they pulled on their clothes, he asked her his questions. She knew of Burl Kerr. He was a lawyer in town who worked for some of the mine owners. She had met him a few times, but didn't know a lot about him. He had an office in the first building this side of A Street and Main. She had never been inside.

"Do you remember Lawson Blaine?"

"Sure, nice man. I never bedded him. He wanted to one night back before he got married, but then we got busy with the supper trade and Joey wouldn't let me have a half hour off. I really wanted him. He was a wonderful guy, and I had designs on him myself. Once Lawson got married, he was faithful to his wife. What a beauty she is. She's got grapefruit under her blouse bigger than mine."

Ki reached out and fondled her breasts. "These will do just fine for me," he said. "Any reason you've heard why Lawson might have been murdered?"

"Murdered? I thought it was an accident. Caught between ore cars. It's happened before, but usually down in the mine a ways, where it's dark. Murdered? Brand-new idea to me. I did hear something about him once. Don't remember if it was before or after he was . . . killed. One of my customers mentioned his name softly to another man. Not sure who it was." She wrinkled her brow trying to remember.

"Oh, yes, now I know which customer it was. He pinched my bottom twice while I was serving him. He wanted me out here on the cot, but I didn't give him a chance to ask."

"You know his name?"

"Sure. The gent you asked about, Burl Kerr. He was the one who mentioned Lawson's name to somebody. As I remember the man was young and wore rough clothes like a miner, and Kerr paid for dinner for both of them."

"Any idea who the second man was?"

17

"Nope. Don't remember seeing him before or since. But there's a lot of people in town I never see. Some always eat at home; some come and are gone a week later."

Happy looked at the small pocket watch she wore on a silver chain around her neck. "Lord a-mighty, I got to go. Joey gonna be pissed that I took so long."

"He knows?"

"Sure. He's the boss. He gets his on Thursday nights. That's when his wife goes out to learn to play bridge. Dumb game, but she likes it, and Joey gets his rocks cracked that way good once a week. What the hell. It's all part of the job."

Ki kissed both her breasts through the soft fabric, and she moaned. "You come back tonight about eight, and we'll go to my place for an all-nighter. I want to see if I can keep up with a Japo like you all night."

She laughed, hurried to the door into the kitchen, and was gone.

Ki checked his clothes, stepped out into the alley, saw no one watching, and walked out to the street and back to the hotel. He and Jessie had not set up a meeting place, but the lobby seemed to be ideal.

When he got there, he found Jessie sitting on a sofa reading a magazine. She had changed into her riding clothes: a pair of cut-down men's jeans, the same blouse, now covered with a denim jacket, and her riding boots.

She nodded and Ki eased down beside her. He told her what he'd found out about Burl Kerr.

"Let's go for a ride," Jessie said. "I have directions to get to the Ready Relief mine."

The mine was out on Chariot Creek, almost on the edge of the desert. It took them an hour and a half to make the ride, but after backtracking once and asking at another mine, they came to the small office building at the Ready Relief.

The hills were cut clear of any kind of timber big enough to be used as shoring or bracing in the mine. The constant hammering of the stamp mill on the creek came through clearly, and Jessie saw that it was powered by a strange-looking overshot waterwheel.

A man came out of the office and stared at them.

18

"Something you want, or are you just tourists out looking at the strange native population?" the man asked.

Jessie swung down from her horse and walked it over to the large man with a rotund belly, a businessman's suit, and a soft white face. She figured him to be about forty-five years old, overweight, and he probably snored.

"I'm looking for Judge Washington Maxwell," Jessie said.

"Guess you've found him," the man said. "Who are you and what do you want?"

"Sir, this is Miss Jessica Starbuck, owner of the Circle Star ranch in Western Texas," Ki said. He stayed mounted, with his right hand hooked into one of his vest pockets, a fraction of an inch from one of his throwing stars.

"Never heard of you or the ranch," Maxwell said. He bowed and waved at his office. "You might as well come in out of the chill. Looks like fall is coming a bit early this year."

Jessica and Ki tied their horses to a rail and went into the small building. Inside three clerks worked on their books. At the back they found a private office, where Maxwell seated the two visitors.

"Hot coffee?" he asked.

They shook their heads.

"Mr. Maxwell, Lawson Blaine worked for me on my ranch for six years. He was the best cowhand I ever saw. Now I understand that he's dead, and I want to help out his widow and do anything I can. Just how did Lawson die? I understand it was here at the mine."

When Jessie mentioned Lawson's name, she saw a slight tightening of Maxwell's mouth, and his eyes closed a fraction of an inch. He regained his former attitude quickly.

"Not a lot I can tell you. I was in town at the time. Evidently he was out checking on the ore cars near the stamp mill and stood in front of one, and because of the noise the mill makes, he didn't hear or see the second loaded ore car rolling down the tracks.

"We make the grade slightly downhill so the cars are easier to push. The stamp mill is somewhat lower so we can use gravity instead of muscle to get the ore into the stamp mill box."

"Did anyone see the accident?" Jessica asked. "Someone

must have been with the second ore car."

"Well, that's the problem, Miss Starbuck. Usually there's two men pushing those ore cars. You saw one coming in. They're only about four feet long and three feet wide or so, and near three feet deep, but they weigh almost a ton when full and take some handling. This time there was one at the end of the tunnel waiting to get pushed out. The two miners shoving the car behind that one didn't see it and rammed right into it, sending it rolling down the incline.

"Happens all the time. There's a removable stop out about fifty feet from the end of the tracks, so the ore car can't get all the way to the stamp mill before they need it."

"So nobody saw the accident that killed Lawson?"

"I'm afraid not, Miss Starbuck. Mining is dangerous work. We have accidents here all the time. We try to keep it as safe as possible, but there are so many chances for something to go wrong. A missed step, a small error in judgment, and a man can die in these mines."

"I understand that, Mr. Maxwell, but this was at night as I understand it and on the surface. I own two coal mines in Wyoming. We've never had anyone severely injured on the surface. How did this happen?"

Maxwell stood. His soft white face had turned hard and flushed with angry blood. "Miss Starbuck, that's why they're called accidents. If we knew why it happened we could make sure it never did again. Now, if you'll excuse me, I have a lot of work to get done."

"Your men took Mr. Blaine's body to the undertaker?" Ki asked.

"That's right. No need for a doctor. He was dead when one of my men found him. I figure they got to him about two hours after he was hit. Now I must ask you to leave."

"Could we talk to the first man who found Lawson?" Jessie asked. "I'm trying to console the widow, and the more I can tell her, the better she can live with the tragedy."

"Wish I could let you talk to him, but that was Newt Jamison, and he's on the day shift now. He's four or five hundred feet underground today, working on a good-looking fold of gold-bearing quartz."

20

Ki looked at Jessie. She nodded slowly. "In that case, Mr. Maxwell, we'll have to catch him when he gets home tonight. I hope we haven't put you out any. Mrs. Blaine is still terribly upset about all of this."

Maxwell's mood changed. He nodded, his face full of concern. "I can understand that. We did pay her two weeks' wages as a death benefit. Blaine was a good man. I was sorry to lose him."

He walked them to the front door and then waved as they moved to their mounts. They stepped into the saddles and rode.

Ki angled his horse closer to Jessie's. "Don't look back," he said, "and don't make any sudden moves. There are at least three rifles or shotguns tracking us. What in hell is going on out here?"

★
Chapter 3

"Rifles tracking our backs?" Jessie asked, the surprise showing in her voice.

"I saw one and I can sense the others. The one rifleman wasn't trying all that hard to be secretive about it."

"Is this just normal security around a gold mine?" Jessica asked. Then she shook her head and answered her own question. "No, not reasonable. When two strangers come up to a gold mine peaceably, you don't automatically put them under the gun."

Ki's face remained impassive, but he shook his head slowly. "Something is wrong back at that mine, Jessie. The root of the trouble, and the why of Lawson's death, is back there somewhere."

"We need to know a lot more about the situation here," Jessie said. "We have a start with this Burl Kerr. We can't go see him at once, that would be a tip-off that we suspect something. Tomorrow I'll call on him for some advice about investing in mines in the Julian area. Somebody is always ready to sell. If you can find Kerr tonight, maybe it would be useful if you followed him. To find out how he is involved in all this."

They rode in silence for a ways.

"I wish I knew about geology," Ki said. "There must be something about the mine or how they're running it that isn't right."

"Maybe Lawson saw or heard about some scheme or scam, and they couldn't count on his silence, so they killed him."

"No blood around the crushing," Ki said. "The undertaker was surprised about that. It means he must have been already dead and held in place when the ore car rammed into him."

"That would take at least two, maybe three men," Jessie said. "A lot of mouths to keep shut. In his quickness to answer about who found the body, Maxwell might have slipped and used a name of one of the men who did the deed."

"Newt Jamison. I'll find out where he lives and meet him as soon as he comes off his day shift," Ki said.

"When we get these horses put away at the livery, I think I'll see if the Julian General Store is still open," Jessie said. "The postmistress usually knows a little about everybody in town. I'm looking for another honest person I can talk to about why we're here."

An hour later Jessie found the postmistress getting ready to close up the store. Jessie slipped inside and bought a new neckerchief to go with her denim outfit.

The woman behind the counter was no more than five feet tall, with soft gray hair bound up in a bun at the back of her neck. She took the thirty cents for the purchase and handed the scarf to Jessie.

"You're a right pretty woman, but I don't see no wedding band. That mean you're still single?" She said it with such honesty and friendliness that Jessie chuckled.

"It does. My name is Jessica Starbuck, and I'm from west Texas."

The small woman held out a wrinkled hand. "Pleased to meet you, Miss Starbuck. My grandmother's name was Jessie. I'm partial to the name. Oh, I'm Yetta Quentin. Me and my husband run the store here. He does opening and mornings, and I do afternoons and closing."

They shook hands.

"You find the widow Blaine?"

23

"I did. Thanks. Now I'm looking for some more information. Can I be frank with you, Mrs. Quentin?"

The small lady laughed and went forward and locked the front door. She pulled down the window shade that said "Sorry, Closed" on it.

When she came back, she jumped up and sat on the counter. "I might be sixty-one, but I'm not dead yet. I didn't figure you were in town for your health." She pursed her lips and turned and spit into a cuspidor near a post. The tobacco juice hit the container in the center.

"Lawson Blaine. Nice boy. I liked him. Figure now that you don't go along with that accident idea of the way he died. Right?"

"Right, Mrs. Quentin."

"No, no. Call me Yetta. All my friends call me Yetta, and I figure you and me can be friends. Murder. Mmmmmmm. Hadn't thought a lot about it. Men get killed in these mines all the time. Damned dangerous way to make a living."

"Why would somebody kill Lawson?" Jessie asked.

"Two reasons most probable. Lawson saw or knew something that he shouldn't. Or else he did something that the powers that be out there at Ready Relief mine didn't like and figured threatened them."

"What in the world could that be?"

"Ready Relief is owned by a syndicate of eight or ten men in San Diego. They like to see profits. It's hit some staggering rich veins lately; then they tapered off, or so the talk goes. Lots of places for gold to slip through the cracks of an organization before the profits show up."

"That certainly would be a good reason to kill a man."

"You need to talk to a fella here in town who's the expert on these mines. About your age, I'd say. Came in from Sacramento as a consultant on the hard-rock mines. Good man. Honest as a good chaw of 'backy. Name of Vince Hirlbach. Works late. Take him to supper and talk his ears off." The small woman giggled. "Oh, he's also handsome and single. His office is just a block down, second floor over the woman's wear store."

Jessie thanked Yetta and shook her hand at the front door.

24

A block down, she found the woman's wear shop and the stairs leading upward. She saw a light in the window, so she walked up the steps.

His name was on the door on a painted wooden sign, with the words "Mining Consultant" under it.

Jessie knocked, then tried the handle. It was unlocked, so she turned the knob and pushed inward.

The office was nicely furnished, with a polished hardwood floor, fancy paper on the walls, and a man standing behind a big cherry wood desk.

"Yes, may I help you?" the man asked.

Jessica closed the door and walked forward into the light with which three lamps showered the room.

"Yes, I think you can help me."

The man behind the desk sucked in a quick breath. "Jessica Starbuck, is it really you?"

Jessie looked up in wonder. He could have found out her name from the hotel, or . . . There was a faint stab of recognition, but it flaked away into dust.

"Yes, I'm Jessie Starbuck, from west Texas. I'm afraid you have the advantage of me, sir."

He was tall, and he wore a brown suit, matching tie, and white shirt. His full blond hair was combed back but straggled here and there. His square, rugged face was clean-shaven, and indeed he was more than handsome, but Jessie couldn't place him.

"Miss Starbuck, pardon me for staring, but you're more beautiful than I remember. We met once two or three years ago in Rock Springs, Wyoming. We worked out some problems on one of your coal mines; then you were off quickly for San Francisco on the train."

"Rock Springs, yes, vaguely. It was such a quick stop. As I recall we were there no more than four hours, and you had the problem well in hand."

"Thank you. Now, is there something I can do for you here in Julian? I didn't even know you owned any of the gold mines here."

"I don't, but there's something you can help me with. I'll be glad to pay you for your time."

25

"No charges. It would be an honor." He looked at the gold watch he had pulled from a vest pocket. "I'd say the first order of business is some supper, or dinner as some call it now. Would you have some dinner with me, Miss Starbuck?"

Jessie smiled. He was attractive, and so charming. She couldn't remember him from Wyoming, but he must have been there. She nodded. "Yes, dinner, but only if you call me Jessie."

"Done, Jessie. We don't have any San Francisco–quality restaurants here in Julian, but I think we can find something that will interest you."

They went almost to the end of two-block Main Street, to a little place called Mama's Cafe. It had only four booths and three tables and was filled except for one booth for two. They slid into the seats, and a large woman in an apron, with wild red hair shooting out from her head in several directions, came rushing out and planted a kiss on Vince's forehead.

"Now, Vince, I hope you've been eating enough. I haven't seen you in three days. By all the saints in heaven I hope you ain't trying to cook for yourself again. What'll you and the lady have tonight?"

"Two of your best, Mama, and all the trimmings. This is a lady from Texas, so she knows good beef when she bites into it."

Mama Lorenzo nodded briefly at Jessie, but it was obvious she was delighted to see Vince. She swept away, brought them back large mugs filled with scalding hot coffee, and hurried off again.

They sipped the coffee.

"You don't order, just take whatever she brings you?" Jessie asked.

"Interesting, isn't it? They do that in some New Orleans restaurants. Most of those are famous for only one dish. If you go there, they bring that specialty to you in seven courses. Mama isn't quite so inventive, but she has just one main dinner each night.

"It can be something of a surprise, depending on what her hunter son brings in with his rifle, but it's always interesting. One night it was two roast quail. Another time it was venison

26

steak, and I've had bear meat here and once a surprise, rattle-snake steak."

"I'll pass on that one unless I'm really hungry," Jessie said.

"Usually the main dish is more conservative, like Mulligan stew or steak or once in a while fresh fish up from San Diego."

He watched her a moment. "You said you had some questions for me?"

"Yes, if now's a good time. I know nothing about gold mining. Can you fill me in on what they have here? It's hard-rock mines with shafts and tunnels—outside of that I'm a stranger."

"You want some geology mumbo jumbo, I can fill it in for you, Jessie. It might be handy for whatever you have in mind.

"Most of the gold mines here in Julian are in irregular schist deposits about a mile wide and six miles long. These gold deposits are of a hydrothermal origin, with small amounts of mineral-bearing rock forced into minute fissures. This happened under tremendous pressure. When this rock cooled and hardened, it became white quartz veins.

"Centuries and centuries of wind and weather eroded the soil from the tops of these veins, and since they were harder than the other rock, they became exposed as upthrusts and signaled that here was a chance for gold in the quartz lower down."

"So you find the white quartz and maybe a gold mine?" Jessie asked.

"Maybe. Usually the quartz on the surface has little if any gold in it, but just where the quartz vein might travel underground is a problem. Nature had the last word here. It shifted the rock masses and caused the layers of quartz to move as much as a mile from their original positions. Then there are fault lines all over the area to further complicate matters.

"A rich vein of quartz might suddenly end, with no chance on knowing which direction to dig to find it again. In the Eagle mine, right near town, the veins of gold-bearing white quartz occur about every fifty feet through the mountain. This mine has veins from an inch to a foot wide and isn't a big producer.

27

The veins usually run at an angle of about sixty degrees, which makes for more problems."

"What about the Ready Relief mine out near the desert?" Jessie asked.

"That one has been a consistent producer and one of the biggest strikes in the whole area. Out there they have a strange situation. In places there are high concentrations of ore, some yielding as much as $500 a ton. One limited area made history when it produced $250,000 of gold to a ton of ore. I'm not sure if they took out just a ton of that ore or most of it."

"So it's a highly profitable mine?" Jessie asked.

Mama returned with two large plates. On each one was a slab of prime rib that must have been an inch thick and ten inches across.

"Mama, you couldn't have done better tonight," Vince said and kissed her cheek. She returned with family-style bowls of potatoes and gravy, horseradish sauce, green peas, carrots, and two vegetables Jessie was not sure what to call.

"Let's eat first and talk more about the Ready Relief later," Jessie said. She tore into the roast beef, smeared on the horse-radish sauce, and found it had been diluted only a little. She yelped and reached for a glass of cold water that Mama had provided.

When the food was gone, Jessie probed about the Ready Relief again.

"Is that the kind of mine that's worth fighting over?"

"It's been a consistent producer even during the lean years here in Julian. It's a strange combination of geological happenings.

"The veins of quartz are huge, some fourteen feet wide. Compare that with the one-inch- to one-foot-wide veins in the Eagle mine. These wide ledges are the result of what is called rolls.

"Geologists have concluded that the compression on the schists at a right angle to one line formed a pressure that resulted in a reverse fault beside a normal one. This pressure crumpled the vein and turned it back on itself so several original veins came together to form the large shelves of ore. The thickness of some of these folds are from twelve to twenty feet.

"The Ready Relief has been sold at least twice that I know of and is still working, evidently, under the command of Washington Maxwell."

Jessie sipped the last of her second cup of coffee and nodded at the geologist.

"Thanks for the lesson. I needed to know. Now, I have another question for you, which I hope you won't tell anyone about. Do you have any idea why Lawson Blaine died out at the Ready Relief about two weeks ago?"

Vince frowned, and it made his face even more attractive, Jessie thought as she watched him. He took a deep breath.

"No, nothing definite. I knew Lawson. We got to talking once before he got married, and I knew that he had worked on your ranch in Texas. I told him I'd met you in Wyoming. He almost told me something about a month ago when we were talking about mines. He was in town on an errand for the mine, and we met on the street and stopped for coffee. He seemed upset about something, but never said what it was. I had the notion it was about the mine where he worked."

"Too bad he didn't tell you. I've a hunch whatever it was caused him to be murdered."

"What?" Vince asked. "The word around town was that he died in an accident."

"His widow thinks he was murdered, and after talking with Maxwell, so do I. All I have to do is figure out how to prove it."

"I can't help you there. I'm no detective."

"Neither am I, but I'm learning," Jessie said. "There's sure no help from the local law, or the county sheriff. My friend and I will just have to stumble around until we dig up something."

"Could that be dangerous?"

"Already has been. Ki was shot at this morning after he talked to the undertaker about Lawson's death. Some fool missed from thirty yards with a rifle, and Ki caught him."

"Was he a hired gun, a drifter?"

"Right, and we're not sure why he was hired, but we have a name of the man who might have hired him."

"A small lead. Look, I'm not terribly busy at the moment. Anything I can do to help you, I'd be glad to do."

29

Jessie smiled. "I just might take you up on that. It's dark out. How about walking me back to the hotel?"

In the lobby, Jessie toyed with the idea of asking Vince to see her to her room, but pushed it aside. She shook his hand, thanked him, and said that if she needed some help, she would be sure to knock on his office door.

She picked up two messages from her key box at the clerk's desk. Both from Ki.

"Hi, I'm conducting a special night research project that might be productive, and then again might not. See you for breakfast in the morning at that same cafe where we ate before. Seven o'clock?"

The other note had been written earlier.

"Found where Newt Jamison lived. His boardinghouse lady said he was usually there by 5:30. I waited until 7:00 and he hadn't come. She said that was highly unusual. Newt was as punctual as clockwork. She checked his room and said that all of his clothes and belongings were gone. No note or letter, and he was behind in his board and room payments. Having checked the livery, my guess is that Newt left town in a rush."

Jessie went to her room after reading the notes. She wished now that she had invited Vince to join her. There was nothing productive she could do tonight. Another talk with the widow Blaine would be of little value. She unlocked her door and pushed it hard so it swung wide and hit the wall. Then she struck a match on her boot sole and held the bright flame inside the room.

No one was there. She lit the lamp on the dresser and closed and locked the door.

Things were starting to pile up. What happened to the man who Maxwell said had been the first one to find Lawson Blaine after the "accident"? Had Maxwell paid him to leave town in a rush? Why had Maxwell been so touchy today at the mine? Just who was this Burl Kerr, and how did he fit into the picture?

Jessie wrote down the three problems in a notebook she took from her traveling bag. Writing them down helped her to sort them out. She needed more facts; she had to go see this Kerr gentleman. She would pretend to be looking for a mine to buy.

30

Kerr sounded like their best lead so far. Did he hire the man to shoot at Ki, and was it because of Lawson's murder? The questions kept pounding at Jessie. She opened her small leather case and looked at several bits of business correspondence. Nothing was so vital it had to be done today. There was that sawmill in Seattle she would have to handle sooner or later. The import/export company in San Francisco had a top manager. She'd wire him some suggestions. She put the leather case away and thought about going down to the dining room for a cup of coffee. It was far too early to go to bed.

She had just decided to go for coffee when a knock sounded on her door. Jessie frowned. It was not Ki's special signal. She went to the locked door, wishing there was a window in it.

"Who is it?" she called.

"Burl Kerr," a heavy voice said. "It's terribly important that I see you right away, Miss Starbuck."

Surprise flooded Jessie's mind. What in the world? "We've never met, Mr. Kerr."

"I know, but this can't wait, Miss Starbuck. We have to talk tonight."

Jessie caught up the reticule with her derringer in it and held it with the top partly open as she unlocked the door.

31

★

Chapter 4

Jessie opened her hotel room door an inch and looked out. A man stood there in the shadows of the poorly lighted hallway.

"What do you want?" Jessie asked.

"We have to talk. I can't do it out here. May I come in? You can leave the door open."

She could see only the tall figure. He appeared sparse, too thin, like a stick figure. Jessie put her hand inside her reticule and gripped the derringer. Then she opened the door and stepped back.

When Burl Kerr entered the room, she saw him plainly for the first time. He wasn't thin; he was skeletal. Sallow skin pulled tightly across his cheekbones. His eye sockets had shrunken to deep, dark holes, and his jaw showed little more than bone with skin tightly wrapped over it. His hands resembled claws.

Jessie kept from gasping with an effort. Kerr stepped behind the door and held it nearly closed with one hand.

"Please don't be alarmed. I am not here to hurt you. By now you must know that I hired a man to shoot near Ki to frighten him. I did not try to have him killed. It's hard to miss with a rifle from thirty yards."

"Your hired gunman could have been killed. Why did you want to scare Ki?"

"With the hope that both he and you would leave town quickly. I lived in Texas for a time. I know of your ranch and your wide international holdings. I feared you might be here to buy a gold mine I'm interested in.".

"I'm not a gambler, Mr. Kerr. A gold mine is the ultimate gamble. Too much risk, too many complications and differentials. I prefer coal in my mining operations. Does that relieve your fear?"

"Partly." Kerr let go of the door and changed his hat to the other hand. He shifted his weight from one foot to the other. He looked at the window, at the bed, and then quickly away.

"What else is troubling you, Mr. Kerr?"

"There are things here you don't understand. Forces at work that have nothing to do with you, but in which you could become involved. You knew Lawson Blaine. My best advice to you is to let it lie. Nothing you do now can bring back the dead, but it could create massive problems, and undoubtedly more men would die."

"So you know as I do, that someone murdered Lawson Blaine. I want to find out who did it and why."

"I can't answer either question for you. I'm only on the fringes of this town. I've been here five years, so I'm still a newcomer. It's a tightly knit community; most of the important people here go back to the first strikes in '70 and '71."

"What could Lawson have found out that was important enough to make someone kill him and cover it up as an accident?" Jessie asked.

"I'm not sure, Miss Starbuck, but I'm certain that I don't want to know. Then I, too, would be in peril. I'm not only representing myself. I work with several of the largest merchants in town. They all have authorized me to urge you to let the matter of Lawson Blaine lie and to move on to your other pressing business."

"Who are these merchants trying to run Ki and me out of town?"

"I'm a lawyer, Miss Starbuck, so that's a confidential lawyer-client matter. I can tell you that we're concerned about the

33

mines. Back in '76 the mines were almost worked out and most shut down. Julian went from two thousand people down to less than a hundred. We don't want that to happen again."

"I'm only here to see justice done, Mr. Kerr. If your committee turns the man or men who murdered Lawson Blaine over to the county sheriff in San Diego, then I'll gladly await the trial in San Diego."

The skeletal man shook his head. "That's not possible. We don't know who killed Blaine. Besides we have no police powers. We sincerely hope that this matter is closed."

"It hasn't even started to open up yet, Mr. Kerr. Did you know that the man who first found Lawson dead has left town without a howdy-do-good-bye to anyone? He left town suddenly or died somewhere; we're not sure which."

"Now you can understand what I mean about your stirring this up. Only more violence can result."

"Tell that to the men who killed Lawson. We're coming after them, and we won't stop until they have met their Maker one way or the other, legal or by 'accident.' "

Burl Kerr stared hard at Jessie a moment, then put on his gray town hat, turned, and went out of the room. He closed the door gently. Jessie locked it at once and frowned trying to figure out his real purpose.

He was afraid of someone, something. Half the merchants in town were afraid of something. What?

Two hours later, and less than a block from where Jessie had at last dropped off to sleep in her hotel room, Sally Wondersome sat at the bar in the Tall Saloon, on a high stool reserved for her. Sally was not one of the dance-hall whores who prowled the back poker tables and gave away quick feels to advertise.

She sat on the stool in a ball gown worth two months of a miner's pay. She had an arrangement with Grandy Tall that she could work his saloon and take her gentlemen friends to her place or to a hotel. She gave Grandy a dollar each night to "rent" the stool. That included a free beer whenever she wanted one.

Sally was pretty, a knockout compared to the whores around the back tables. She paid attention to her face and her figure, and ate enough to stay alive but thin and nurture her full breasts. She had cherry red hair, a deep, beautiful shade that was her trademark and her passion. She washed it every morning and combed and brushed it until it shone. At twenty-four years, Sally had spent seven of them as a prostitute and now was at the top of the trade. She asked for, and had no trouble selling her time for, ten dollars an hour.

"Best fucking hour you'll ever have," she said softly into the ear of a man who had been talking to her for five minutes. He'd bought her a whiskey and had his hand on her knee, but she cracked his knuckles, warning him that that was all he could have free.

More than once a night some wide-eyed young boy or a drunk came up to her at the stool with a note. Sometimes it was an envelope with a ten-dollar bill inside and an invitation to come out to a carriage or a hotel room. Sally prided herself on giving full value for her services. She claimed that she'd never had an unhappy client in her life.

Grandy Tall, behind the mahoganbar, pattered down the bar toward her. As a true midget, Grandy stood just three feet tall, with a perfectly proportioned body. He owned the Tall Saloon and had erected a permanent platform in back of the bar so he could move back and forth, serve drinks, make change, and get a good look at the whores working the back tables.

Grandy served the best whiskey in town and tolerated no fighting. He had a huge Chinese man named Lou How who appeared in seconds when any kind of a dispute began. His six-foot-six and 350-pound presence instantly defused arguments. When it didn't, he picked up the combatants, one under each massive arm, and carried them to the street, where he delighted in dropping them in fresh cow pies made by the many teams of oxen that pulled freight wagons in and out of town.

Grandy grinned at Sally and handed her an envelope. She moved the ranch hand's hand from her knee. She knew he didn't have ten dollars. Sally tore open the envelope and read the short note. It said only: "J. Downing, office. Now."

She smiled. That's how J. Downing did business. Behind his own closed doors. No wonder he held the title as the second richest man in town. Besides he usually came across with a ten-dollar tip for services.

"Buck, when you can come up with the ten good U.S. dollars, you come calling. Right now I have a business appointment. Don't give up hope, dear boy. You'll never forget an hour with Sally Wondersome." The cowboy sagged in disappointment. "Hey, range rider, if'n you got a dollar and a half, you talk to Flossy back there. She'll let you poke her for that much, and it's about what she's worth. Go see her."

Sally slid off the stool. She stood little more than five feet tall, but packed a fine body into that height. She waltzed her way to the door. As she said, it never hurt to advertise, even when there was no good client watching. You never knew.

A few minutes later Sally knocked on a door over the real estate office. The door showed the lettering "J. Downing Clatter, Attorney At Law." Sally pushed the door open and walked in. As usual, she found no one in the outer office. She grinned. This damned J. Downing must be playing games again. She locked the front door with the twist mechanism, dropped her reticule on the nearest chair, and went to the only door that led off the office.

As soon as she pushed it open, a whip cracked beside her. Her eyes widened as she looked up and saw the lawyer dressed all in black and wearing a dark mask as he pulled back the whip.

"Woman, I told you to come. Now get over here before I make nasty whip marks on that soft white flesh."

"J. Downing, you know if you make one mark on me, I'll take out my derringer and blow two new holes through your forehead. This gonna be a quick game or one lasting all night? It's fifty dollars for all night."

"Fer Chrissakes, Sal, you know it's just an hour. Now, let's play the game before my time's up. I can't afford no fifty-dollar pokes."

She unbuttoned the fasteners down the front of the ball gown, letting her breasts pop out. J. Downing dropped the whip and rushed over to help her undress.

36

"Hell, Sal, you got to play the game or it isn't any fun."

"Sure, JD. Sure. Now what's the big deal you're working on? Who do you want me to question when I've got him with his privates hanging out?"

"Judge Washington Maxwell, who else? He's working something, and I can't find out what it is. Killed that guy, Blaine. He must have heard or seen something he wasn't supposed to. Blaine worked in the final casting room where the bars of gold are poured. Something big is about to happen around this quiet little mining town, and I want to know what it is as soon as possible."

"Maybe it's the fancy prancy who came to town today."

"You referring to Jessica Starbuck? She's got so much money and businesses all over the world I don't see why she doesn't go spend some of her cash and buy a ship and sail around the world or something." Clatter caught Sally's bare breasts and nibbled on them.

For the first time she saw the ropes and leather harness attached to the ceiling and hanging over the small bed at the side of the room.

"What the hell is that thing?"

"You'll find out. Now, what about Maxwell? You used to do him every Thursday night at his town house. Why don't you go over there tonight and seduce the old bastard?"

"He said he was tired of me."

"That was two months ago. A man doesn't get tired of perfection, sweet lady. He had some other reason. Go over and offer him a free one and get him talking."

"I don't do free."

"I'll pay for an hour. Then you get your pretty little ass right back here and tell me every blessed word that he said. Get him talking about the mine, about his production. Bait him. Tell him that the Stonewall is going at six hundred dollars a ton."

"It ain't. He'd know that's a lie."

"Tell him something."

By then both of them had stripped out of their clothes. J. Downing motioned Sally over to the bed.

"What is this contraption?"

37

"You always want to be on top. This way you climb in the harness facedown, and I lower you as far as I want, to nibble and chew and eat anything I want to."

"No hurting, my rule. Nothing that hurts, or it costs you a thousand dollars."

"I know, I know. This will hold you. I climbed in it myself. Now get up there and let's see what kind of fun we can have for the rest of my hour."

Sally wasn't amused. The contraption got in the way, and even when he lowered her into a fitting position, it just wasn't as good as usual. After a half hour she slid out of the slings and harnesses and put on her clothes.

"No more of these damn specials, JD, or it's going to cost you a hundred. I didn't like that thing. Never again."

J. Downing shrugged. "Hell, I'll give most anything a try. You remember your assignment. I want you to find out what the hell is going on out at that damn Ready Relief mine. Maxwell is the key. You get him between your legs, and he'll tell you everything he knows. The man is an idiot."

"But he's richer than you are, JD. Even with your piddling little gold mine at two ounces a ton."

"The Minerva is doing better. At what I paid for it, anything I take out is damn near all profit."

"I know all about your sneaky ways, JD. Just don't use them on me. I'll try to get to Maxwell, but not sure if I can. I can always invite myself over on Thursday night and try to pretend I'd forgotten he cut me off."

"Great idea. Today is Wednesday. You have all day tomorrow to make yourself beautiful."

"I'm always beautiful, you horse's ass," Sally said. She fastened the last button on her dress, leaving a generous portion of cleavage showing, then started for the door.

Clatter beat her there and pushed a twenty-dollar gold piece down between her breasts. "Just so you don't forget about Maxwell," he said. She retrieved the double eagle, grinned, and hurried out into the night.

How was she going to play this, how? Maxwell was no fool. If she suddenly showed up, he'd be on his guard. He always had something dirty or rotten working. Why didn't he just tend

38

to his gold mine and let the rest of the town alone? Not the way Washington Maxwell worked. Not his style at all. If he had a million dollars, he'd still try to steal a fifty-cent piece off a drunk. Yes, that would be the Maxwell style. He figured everyone anywhere near smart must be crooked like him.

Slowly a smile spread over Sally's face. She came through the alley door of the Tall Saloon and hurried to the bar. She winked at Grandy Tall as he polished some glasses behind the mahogany bar. The little guy amazed her. She'd given him a couple free ones early on.

By the time she slid onto her stool at the end of the bar, Sally had worked out her plan. Yeah, it could work. She would play both ends against the middle. She'd spy on Maxwell and all the time make out like J. Downing Clatter was setting up a scheme to rope in Maxwell. Hell, she would get paid by both sides!

Sally's mood brightened just thinking about it, and when Grandy brought her a cold beer, she bent over the bar and kissed his forehead.

Grandy grinned, watched her a moment, then rubbed his fly. "Sweet Sally, you ain't paid the rent yet this month. Wasn't that the agreement we had, once a month in the back room?"

"That agreement sort of petered out, Grandy. But tonight I feel so good I'd be more than happy to service you. How about right now before I get involved with somebody?"

Grandy yelped his pleasure and bellowed for his partner, Hightower, to come mind the bar. Then the little man vanished through the door at the far end of the bar.

Five minutes later Sally had finished her beer. She slid off the bar, letting her skirt ride up past her knee. Three miners panted openly as they watched from the front table. She winked at them, then walked behind the bar and through the back door into a large room where Grandy lived. He already had his pants off.

"Hey, didn't know if you were coming, so I started without you," Grandy said. It was a standing joke between them.

Outside the room, in the saloon, a bearded man with a hat pulled low over his eyes stared into his beer. He had seen her come and go once; now she had gone into the back room. He could wait. His boss had said he wanted to see her tonight.

He'd deliver the note, and if that didn't work, it simply meant he had to kidnap her, get her on a horse, and take her by force to the boss. Not a bad package to have to paw around a little.

He knew her, a high-society-girl whore, pretending to still be in Boston or something. He might just do her himself on the way out to the boss. Who would know the difference?

Yeah, who would know, just the slut. No problem there. The boss said to bring her any way he could. He was supposed to get her to the office by midnight. Lots of time. His lips parted, and two firm teeth showed, sided by two blackened stumps. Yeah, he'd always wanted a nice firm piece like that Sally. Who could afford ten dollars? He'd have his ten dollars' worth for free tonight, and then some. Twelve o'clock? Over two hours away.

★

Chapter 5

Earlier that same evening, Ki had picked up Burl Kerr's trail and followed him as Jessie had suggested. Kerr spent most of his time in his office, but left and made his way to a saloon, where he played cards for a couple of hours. Then he went to a large house on C Street, on the upward slope that gave the place a commanding view of much of Julian.

Kerr went to the rear door and knocked, and soon someone opened it. Ki watched from a safe distance away.

Inside the rear porch Judge Washington Maxwell stared at the visitor.

"What the hell do you want, Kerr?"

"Mr. Maxwell, just my weekly report as usual. Thought you'd like to know that the woman in town with the Japanese man is still nosing around. I had somebody shoot near the Japo, but it didn't scare him off one bit. Told her I was working with the merchants association. She's a tough one, and smart. I'd watch her careful."

"Kerr, you idiot. That's why I pay you to watch her and the other idiots in this stupid little town. What about the Japo?"

"He's half-white, half-Japanese. Evidently they aren't married or anything. He's her bodyguard, her protector. He's a strange one, but he doesn't wear a gun, so I guess he isn't dangerous."

41

Maxwell stood there in the half light, glaring at the shorter man, who looked like a skeleton. "Kerr, it ain't your job to figure out who's dangerous and who ain't. You leave that up to me. Now, get the hell out of here before somebody spots you. I don't take kindly to having everyone know you're working for me. Git!"

Kerr bobbed his head twice, then slipped out the rear door, into the comforting darkness. He could take the verbal abuse from this man. Maxwell had only been in town for three years. He wouldn't last. Burl Kerr would be in Julian, a force in Julian, long after Judge Washington Maxwell was gone and forgotten.

Maxwell watched the thin man vanish in the gloom and snorted softly before he went back to the parlor. It was his favorite room. He had entertained there now and then, but that was when he was new in town and trying to get well established. He didn't need that now.

Maxwell stare into the fire, then read a book. It was near midnight and he had dozed off when he heard someone knock on the rear door. Maxwell marched to the door and flung it open. To his surprise Sally Wondersome stood there scowling. Even in the low light from the front hall he could see that her dress had been torn and her arms were holding the fabric over her breasts. Then he remembered he had asked Rod to bring her to his place tonight.

Sally had her arms crossed, holding up her dress. Maxwell motioned her inside, and Rod came in behind her. The moment the door closed, she screamed at Rod and tore at him, her fingernails raking the air, trying for his face.

"You bastard! You fucking bastard. You raped me. I told you no a dozen times." She turned on Maxwell. "You ordered this dog turd to bring me here? Why him? A nice note to Grandy would get me here faster. Don't ever send this shithead after me again. He threw me down in the grass outside and raped me. The bastard!" She ran at Rod, but Maxwell caught her.

The big man turned to Rod. "You forced yourself on her outside on the lawn?"

"Hell, boss. You said get her here. You said I didn't have

42

to be gentle. Sure I poked her once. Hell, she's nothing but a whore anyway."

Sally spit in his face, and he swung at her with his fist but missed. Maxwell drew the .44 from his side leather and clubbed Rod alongside the head. He staggered back, blood oozing from the scrapes down his head and cheek.

"Rod, get out of here. You're through working for me." Maxwell tossed him a double eagle. "Get out of town. If I ever see your ugly face around Julian again, I'll be shooting to kill you. Understood?"

Rod caught the gold coin in the air and snorted. "Damned whore, anyway. Yeah, I'm going." He shook his head at Sally. "Hell, I've had a better poking from a one-dollar dance hall girl than you give out. You're a nothing." He turned and hurried out the back door into the night.

"The bastard! What did he expect when he raped me?"

"Forget it. You're not exactly virgin material. I know you've been screwing Clatter. What the hell is that slope-headed shyster lawyer up to, anyway?"

"Right now he's trying to buy the Eagle mine. Everyone says it's a low-output hole in the hill, but he wants it. He also has some men out on Crater Creek. He thinks there's another bonanza out there, with some outcroppings of white quartz indicating rich folds below, like you have at the Ready Relief."

"He's crazy. I've walked Crater Creek from one end to the other, and there's nothing there. Not a damned thing. But I'll put four men out there tomorrow just to be sure. What else is he up to?"

"I didn't find out much else. He doesn't talk a lot."

"That's your job, to get Clatter to talk." He watched her a minute. "You look beat up. You want a drink?"

"No, don't feel like it." She glared up at him. "Nor do I feel like getting poked again either, in case you were getting yourself all hard."

Maxwell grunted. "Hey, you don't talk that way with me. You're a whore, a good one, but a whore, and a whore's job is to spread her legs anytime, anywhere."

"I'm not a whore . . ."

43

"Yeah, I know, you're an expensive fancy lady. I remember." He snorted and patted her on her bottom. "Now get the hell out of here, and bring me some important news the next time. I still want you to get over here once a week with the latest on everyone, especially on that bastard J. D. Clatter."

"You have some pins I can fasten this dress together with?"

"I look like a damned seamstress to you? Get out of here." He moved toward the back door, and she went with him.

"Next week, and I won't be sending a note to Tally. He's got a mouth bigger than yours. Beat it!"

Sally took two steps down the stairs at the back of Maxwell's house but missed the last one. She yelped in alarm as she tripped and went down. One knee scraped, and she could feel it burning. Damn! She'd have a bloody knee to explain to everyone. Things hadn't gone well for her today. Double damn. She'd go back to the saloon. Something good might work out yet.

It was just past twelve-thirty when she pushed up onto her stool. The saloon had six men in it, all playing cards. Two of the upstairs girls sat at a back table watching the door. They both shrugged.

Grandy came down the bar and asked if she wanted a beer. She shook her head.

"Just a shoulder to lean on," she said. The midget watched her.

"A tough night? Come on back and let me tell you something, it might help."

"Like what?"

"Come and see."

Sally shrugged. Why not? She slid off the stool and followed the three-foot-high man into the back room. He boosted himself up on the edge of the big bed and patted a place beside him.

"What?" she asked as he stared at her.

"So beautiful. I'm a lucky man to have you now and then. I ever tell you about my mother?"

"No."

"She was an inch shorter than I am. All over San Francisco people knew her. They called her Little Lulu. She was the

44

smallest and highest priced whore in town for ten years. When I got to be ten years old, she quit the business. She said she wanted to raise me right. Three days later, just outside our building, somebody stabbed her to death and stole a fifty-dollar diamond ring off her finger.

"Ten years as a whore and not so much as a skinned knuckle, then, poof, and she was gone. The next day, after her funeral, my father jumped off the tallest building in San Francisco. It turned out to be plenty high enough. I was ten years old and an orphan."

"But you had relatives, people who took care of you?"

"Sure, three whores in a house down near the waterfront. They took care of me, hid me from the cops, helped me grow up, even taught me how to read and write and cipher, but not much else. When I was twelve, they taught me how to make love.

"I worked in the saloon where the girls were. I mopped the floor. I emptied cuspidors. I ran errands. The whores taught me how to steal from the cash drawer so the boss would never know it. He didn't pay me anything, so he owed me. By the time I was fifteen, I had five hundred dollars stashed in a hole in the wall. Then one night I took all of the cash from the money box behind the bar, added my five hundred, and caught a coastal steamer to Portland in Oregon.

"Up there I opened a saloon in a little place, made some money, got run out of town, and worked my way down the coast. You ever wonder how old I am?"

"Yeah, wondered, never asked."

"I'm thirty-two, and the doctor tells me I have a year and a half yet before my heart gives out. A year and a goddamn half!"

Sally reached over and kissed his cheek. "Why didn't you tell somebody?"

"Why, and have you cry? Hell, I want to have a fine time with what days I have left." He reached over and petted her breasts. "Right now I want to try you again. It's been too long since I've done two in one day."

Sally felt better. Her scraped knee didn't hurt. She got a kick out of a poking by this small man. A year and a half!

45

Jeez, what bad luck. Compared to Grandy she was sitting in clover. She had money in a San Diego bank. She was young; she had her looks and a fucking good ass. Yeah, she felt a lot better. Let Maxwell pull her reins around a little. She wasn't in his harness, not anymore. From now on Sally did one thing: She looked out for Sally first.

She reached down and undid Grandy's fly.

"Come on, big man, let's see if we can do at least three more before the sun comes up."

They did.

Back at the Julian Hotel, after Burl Kerr had left Jessie's room, she paced back and forth, thinking about what he had said. She hadn't figured out Kerr yet. If he was truly representing the merchants in town, why would he risk hiring someone to shoot a rifle near Ki? Did he think that would be enough to scare Ki and her away?

She found Kerr's little speech hard to believe. On the other hand, he might have come just to test the waters, to meet her and evaluate her toughness. That could be it. But that still didn't tell her who was he working for.

Ki came by a half hour before midnight, obviously not being able to wait until breakfast to report to Jessie. Jessie put the book to one side as he gave his traditional knock on the door: three quick raps, a pause, and then two more. She let him in.

"I'm not sure about the walking skeleton," Ki said as he sat smoothly in the straight-backed chair. "Kerr spent most of his time in his office. After it was dark for a couple of hours, he left by the front door, had two beers in a saloon, played some cards, and then slipped out the back door and walked down here to the hotel. He came up to the second floor, but I didn't see which room he went in. A short time later he made his way by the back streets to a house I'm told belongs to Judge Washington Maxwell.

"He was inside for maybe ten minutes, then came out, and as I began to follow him, two more persons came to Maxwell's back door. In a flash of light from the lamp inside, I made out the expensive lady who sits on a stool at the Tall Saloon. Her name is Sally, and she charges ten dollars a poke. She doesn't even talk to the dance hall girls in back.

"A man forced her along, then pushed her up the steps and forced her into the house."

Jessie pondered this information. "So, Maxwell has one of the town lawyers under his thumb, but he has to get the fancy lady to his place by force. Doesn't make much sense for now; maybe it will later. Kerr was here to see *me* tonight. What you said just about wipes out what Kerr told me about working for some group of merchants. So he's probably on Maxwell's payroll. That doesn't help us much. Unless Maxwell told him to try to scare you and me out of town."

"That could be," Ki said. "I'll have a talk with the fancy lady tomorrow. Maybe then we can make more sense out of it."

"Let's keep tabs on Kerr and still have your talk with the pretty lady," Jessie said. "Wouldn't be the first time a whore has worked for the big men in town. Sometimes they hear more than they should."

Ki grinned. "Maybe I should go and check on her now. She might be back in the saloon."

Jessie frowned a moment, then laughed. "Tomorrow will do just fine. Let's have breakfast here in the hotel at seven. I want to go talk to the widow lady. She might know more about her husband's death than she realizes."

They said good night, and Ki went to his room, where he spent an hour doing traditional martial arts exercises to keep his body supple, a walking weapon. At the end of the hour he bowed, quickly cleaned the sweat off his body at the washstand bowl, and dried himself. He fell on the bed and went to sleep within thirty seconds.

★

Chapter 6

Jessie awoke at five-thirty in the morning. She lay there working over what she wanted to get done during the coming day, then got up, washed her face, combed her hair, and put on a town dress, so she would blend in more with the other women. She had breakfast with Ki at the hotel dining room.

Jessie thought he was acting keyed up. She smiled at him. "Why are you so full of energy this morning?"

"Today is when I meet the famous Sally Wondersome, the whore with the magic fingers, the fanciest fancy lady in all of Julian. I want to find out what she was doing at the Maxwell house last night. She wasn't there long enough for one of her usual service calls."

Jessie laughed softly. "Remember, she's a professional. She knows how to get men talking. Some of the best spies and confidence people I know have been ladies of the night. Just a small word of warning. Of course, I wouldn't want to restrict in any way the manner in which you do your job."

Ki finished his breakfast and chuckled. "I'll try to protect myself at all times," he said. "As well as find out anything I can to help us discover who killed Lawson."

"I'm on my way out to the widow's house right now," Jessie said. "Sometimes a person knows more than they think they do about a situation like this. What he said those last few weeks might be coming back to her now."

They parted on the hotel steps, and Jessie headed for the widow Blaine's house.

Shortly after eight o'clock she knocked on the widow's door. She heard a flurry of activity inside the house for a moment; then someone called.

"Be there in just a moment," a woman's voice said.

Jessie tapped her foot half a dozen times, turned around on the porch, and stared down the slope to the small town. A moment later Agatha Blaine opened the door. Her hair hung unkempt and mussed; she wore a housecoat and obviously hadn't been out of bed long. A deep blush showed up her neck.

Jessie ignored the telltale signs and smiled.

"Agatha, there are some things I want to ask you. Have I come too early? Would it be better if I came back later?"

"No, no, Jessie. I'm afraid I slept in a bit. I'm about to get some breakfast." She lifted her brows. "Would you like something? Come in. What have you found out so far?"

"I just had breakfast at the hotel. I'm afraid I haven't discovered much yet about who killed your husband, Agatha. I'm hoping that you can help me fill in some blanks."

"Do my best, but as you know, Lawson wasn't much of a talker."

"I remember." They moved into the kitchen, where Agatha lit a fire that had been set in the wood-burning kitchen range. She put on a pot for coffee and then took out an iron fry pan.

"Agatha, any idea what Lawson did before he came here?"

The widow looked up quickly. "Oh, I don't think he was in any trouble, you know, wanted by the law or anything. Nothing like that. He was a good man."

Jessie smiled. She had seen the telltale flush of sexual afterglow at the widow's neck, and she was sure it covered her chest. Jessie knew she had interrupted early morning lovemaking. She wasn't worried about who it had been, even though the widow's husband had been dead less than two weeks. That was Agatha's business—unless it had some bearing on her husband's death.

49

"I remember once in Texas Lawson told me he might be interested in doing some law work," Jessie said. "Did he mention anything about that?"

"Oh, yes, he did, now that you remind me. He said he was a deputy sheriff in some county in Wyoming for a while. Didn't talk much about it. I remember him saying he'd been through so many wanted posters that the men all started looking alike."

She paused, a far-off look on her face. "Oh, then about a month ago or so he did say something about thinking he saw a man here in town who was on one of the wanted posters out of Rock Springs, Wyoming. That's where he worked as a deputy. Said he was going to send the name in a letter back there to the sheriff's office and see if it was the same man.

"He said he figured the man would have changed his name by now, so he sent them a long physical description of the man. Don't rightly know if he ever sent the letter. Lawson wasn't much of one to write letters. He coulda. Don't recollect him ever getting any mail from Rock Springs. Course, usual he picked up the mail from the postmistress. Guess he could have got something from back there in Wyoming and he never showed it to me."

She scowled for a minute. "Nope, for certain he never mentioned it again, one way or the other."

"Interesting," Jessie said. "After Wyoming, where did he go, did he say? It might help us unravel what this mystery is all about."

"He didn't say much more about his wandering. That's what he called it, his two years of wandering, of being a real fiddlefoot. He was in Nevada for a while, and he said he went up the coast on a freighter as a sailor but didn't like that, so he jumped ship in Portland and worked his way back down the coast."

"That could be some good help, Agatha. Now, you told me that he worked in the place where they melted down the amalgam and poured the gold bars. Are there a lot of gold bars made up at the same time? Where do they keep the gold bars, in some kind of safe?"

Agatha tested the skillet, put coffee in the pot to boil, and added some eggshells to help settle the grounds. Then she broke two eggs into the skillet.

"Do a couple for you, Jessie?"

"No, thanks."

"The gold. It was closely guarded, Lawson told me. They would wait until they had a stack of the amalgam from the screens under the stamping mills, then do a batch at a time, maybe every two weeks, he said. It depended how good the deposits of ore were they worked."

"Where did they store the gold bars?"

"Oh, they had a worked-out tunnel that led into the mountain right near the smeltering shed. The amalgam and the finished gold bars both went in there. It was guarded outside and inside twenty-four hours a day, Lawson told me. The guards had orders to shoot to kill and everybody at the mill and in the whole county knew about them. Nobody went near that treasure tunnel."

Jessie stood and walked around the room. It was furnished the way most of the houses in town must have been, with whatever inexpensive items could be found at local or San Diego stores. "How did Lawson get his job with the Ready Relief?"

"Easy. He said he heard they were hiring, and the first day in Julian he went in and asked for a job. Two men had quit that morning, and Lawson went right to work in the smeltering shed. He learned every job in there and soon was the lead man."

"He ever mention how the gold bars were shipped out of Julian?"

"Oh, sure. Everyone knows that. The gold goes by special Wells Fargo strongbox on a stage with several guards. Lately they've been picking up the finished gold bars from all the mines on the same night, and then about two o'clock in the morning the stage roars down the trail toward San Diego."

"Has the shipment ever been robbed?" Jessie asked.

"One time somebody tried. About three years ago, I guess. But the guards shot two of the holdup men dead and wounded and captured the other two. Since then nobody's wanted to try a thing."

51

By then they were sipping the scalding hot coffee. Jessie tried it again. Strong enough to make a spoon stand up straight.

Agatha wiped off the top lid on the wood stove with a cloth, then lay on a slice of homemade bread. She let it toast awhile, then flipped it over with a knife, and soon brought it to the table.

"Toast?"

Jessie shook her head.

"I still can't figure out no reason why somebody would kill Lawson. He was such a good man. His boss, Mr. Maxwell, did give me two weeks' wages, near to fifty dollars, after Lawson's accident. I put it on account with the Julian General Store. We don't have no bank here, so most of us put money with the store. We buy things, and they take the amount off our account. If we need ten dollars cash, we usual can get it from Yetta at the General Store."

"A good arrangement." Jessie paused. "Agatha, who did Lawson work with at the mine? Did he have a best friend, someone who came over to play cards or for dinner, anything like that?"

"We didn't socialize a lot; I was trying to get pregnant. But there was one man he spoke of a lot, Earl Frenken. He was single, about Lawson's age. They both worked in the amalgam smeltering room. I'd say he was about the closest friend who Lawson had here in town or at the mine."

"Earl still works at the mine?"

Agatha nodded. "As far as I know. We had him over for Sunday dinner two or three times. Mostly fried chicken, but he sure liked it. Earl's a good man."

"There's a chance he might know something about the accident. We'll try to get in touch with him. He worked the day shift out at the Ready Relief?"

"Yes. For as long as I can remember."

Jessie stood. "Thanks for this talk, Agatha. Ki and I will do our best to find out what really happened out at the mine. The more I see of this town, the more convinced I am that it wasn't an accident out there. I plan on talking to some more people this morning, Agatha. If you think of anything more, you let me hear from you. I'm at the Julian Hotel."

52

Outside the widow's neat home, Jessie paused a moment to think. She still had nothing. Even the slim lead on Burl Kerr had turned out to be a scare tactic that probably came from Maxwell. It was understandable that the mine owner was thin-skinned about the death of one of his workers. But could there be more to it than that? Jessie headed back downhill, toward Main Street.

A block on down Main, Ki pushed open the batwings of the first saloon he found open. A sign said it was ready for business twenty-four hours a day. It was too early for Ki to want a beer. He talked to the barkeep, who kept polishing the shiny wood in front of him.

"The pretty whore with the big price? Sure, that's Sally Wondersome. She don't work here. She's always at the Tall Saloon, the one the midget runs. Yeah, she's a boomer all right, but costs you half a month's pay to get between her legs. Oh, hell, yes, I think about her every once in a while, but no whore is worth ten bucks for a quick poking."

"She's always at the Tall Saloon, right?" Ki asked.

"Depends how late she worked last night. Most of the whores don't start business hours until late afternoon. I hear that Sally gets on her stool in her pretty dress long about one o'clock in the P.M. If she ain't there, just hang around. That's one fancy whore. She's saved her money, I hear. Don't have to split the take with no madam, and she's independent as hell."

Ki nodded, thanked the apron man, and walked out into the coastal mountain air. It was different here than in Texas. Higher up, the air smelled cleaner and more pure despite two hundred or more smoking chimneys on the slopes in and around Julian.

Today the smoke rose straight into the heavens. It was easy to see where the mines were. The slopes around the shafts and tunnels were cut clear of trees and brush and anything that would burn. The woodcutters had made a rough circle for half a mile around each mine.

Somebody had said that if there were ten more mines discovered in Julian, the wet side of the mountains wouldn't have a single tree left growing, they'd all be deep in the ground, holding up a mine tunnel roof.

Ki hadn't been doing as much running lately as he liked. He wanted to get out into the hills, where he could be alone. He needed to remember that his Americanized name, Ki, came from the Japanese *key-i,* which meant spirit meeting.

Ki had become accustomed to his role in America. He was still a samurai, a soldier/slave to his master, but he was also a half-breed, neither all Japanese nor fully American. His Japanese ancestry meant a great deal to him, but how could he live up to that half of his heritage? He was no Zen master, always serene, totally wise. He had doubts and fears. He must center himself.

Ki ran down the road away from town, into the hills, and up a faint trail that might have been trodden by deer seeking water. Today he felt as if he belonged nowhere. He must strive to bring his spirit into harmony with nature and all things good and pure.

Hundreds of plans, problems, and thoughts tumbled through Ki's mind as his legs pistoned along up the winding trail, branching one way and then the other, always conscious of where he was and how to get back. When his breath came in gulps and gasps from running uphill at this higher altitude, Ki dropped to his knees, closed his eyes, and bowed low until his head touched the softness of the leaf mold under the Jeffrey pine and white oak.

Ki meditated, letting his mind soar, like a morning cloud on a spring day, drifting slowly over the landscape as he watched the tiny mortals below, saw their buildings, watched their cattle and horses.

Then mists covered everything, and a wind whipped up, and the small cloud was torn into tiny fragments that drifted and vanished as the wind ripped them apart.

Raindrops sprinkled Ki. He came up from the bowing position and blinked. It was raining, a mountain shower from a sudden thunderstorm. He could hear the crack of lightning and the crashing together of the air and clouds above him.

He rose, refreshed and renewed, and ran back the way he had come. By the time he entered the hotel, he had covered more than ten miles and was soaked from the rain. He ran up

54

Ki caressed her suddenly warm breasts, then slid one hand down the top of her party dress and curved it around her bare bosom.

"Sally, I've never had the pleasure of loving such a high-class fancy woman."

They both smiled, then sat down and rolled on the bed, and Ki ended up on top. He opened the fasteners on the front of Sally's dress and pulled the cloth back to reveal her breasts. For a moment he sucked in a breath—even lying down, her breasts were large, with three-inch-wide faint-pink areolas around them, tipped with half-inch-long nipples, cherry red and throbbing. He bent and kissed each, then sat up with her, and they undressed each other.

"Usually I don't bother with this seduction kind of thing," Sally said. "But when I first looked at you up close, I praised my stars I sat on that stool. Otherwise I would have fallen down right there. Something about your face, your body, so lean and tough, so sensitive, so downright sexy."

Ki rolled her over so she was on top of him, and she let one breast drop into his mouth. Ki tried to chew it all at once, gave up and nibbled around the edges, then licked her nipple until he could feel it throbbing faster and faster.

Sally shook her head at him and let her long red hair fall down over his face. "Dammit, Ki, I'm not supposed to get all sexy and worked up this way. You could ruin my business outlook."

Ki came away from one breast and shifted to the other one. "Not a chance of ruining your business," he said. "With your looks, your charm, and your amazing body, you could be one of the top parlor girls or 'come home' fancy ladies in San Francisco. You could easily get forty dollars a throw."

Sally's eyes brightened. "You've been there?" He nodded. "You think forty bucks a poke?"

"At the right parlor house and with the right buildup."

Sally squealed in delight, and her slender hips began to thrust at him. She fumbled between their lean bodies, finding his hardness, then lifted a little to aim him at the right spot. She slid down until he was fully impaled in her quivering flesh.

57

"Don't talk, just love me, make it last as long as you can. I want to remember this one. This is the first time in over two years that I've been set on fire by any man. You have that something I just can't get enough of."

Ki stroked upward, slowly at first, then faster, and she shook her head.

"Rest a minute, slow down. You have anything else to do this afternoon?" He shook his head. "So we stay right here until you can't get it up anymore. I want to wear you out and be so sore tomorrow that I'll squeal in pleasure just remembering you."

She held him and squirmed to one side, rolled halfway over, until they both lay on their sides, then wrapped her top leg over his back so her hips stroked against him.

Ki grinned at her comments, matched her thrusts, and soon the rhythm established itself and they panted and moaned as they both worked toward satisfaction. To Ki's surprise, Sally peaked first. A long, low moaning came, followed by a series of harder thrusts and high-pitched squeals as her body spasmed in a series of vibrations and shakings, ending with a roaring bellow of satisfaction, a cry Ki thought must typify the female animal down through the aeons. She went limp for a moment; then her eyes popped open.

"My god, I beat you. I never do that." She rolled over on her back, pinning him in place, and lifted her legs onto him so that she nearly stood on her shoulders.

"Now, big one, finish him off in grand style."

Ki was so near he needed only a dozen strokes in the deep penetration position to crack the world into a million pieces and scatter them into the winds of the universe. He pounded hard at her slender form seven more times before he heaved a sigh of total satisfaction and regeneration and eased down on top of her.

She rolled them to their sides again and nestled her head on his shoulder.

"My god, I don't believe that. You made me feel damned near like a virgin again. How did you do that, Ki?"

"Ancient Oriental secret I can never tell you."

"You're kidding."

"No, let me show you again."

Ki rolled her over, and a moment later he was hard again and thrusting her legs to his shoulders.

"You can't again so fast, Ki. You just finished—My god, you're hard as a pine tree again!"

Ki gripped her shoulders for support and pounded hard and fast, and within a minute he climaxed again, each of his final thrusts jolting her higher and higher on the bed.

She stared at him in amazement, eyes wide and baffled, yet curious.

"Ki, you've got to tell me your secret. What is it?"

He panted a moment, then rolled them to their sides as he rested again.

"We have all afternoon. Perhaps you'll be able to figure out the ancient Japanese secret of making love." He laughed, "But most likely not. I'm only half-Japanese, so I'm twice as careful about telling anyone the long-kept secret."

She stared at him. "Most of that's bullshit, Ki. We both know it, but I'm still curious. Not one man in a thousand can come like that twice in a row. Eventually I'll figure it out."

Ki chuckled. "Not likely. I won't be in town that long."

A few minutes later they sat side by side on the edge of Sally's bed. Ki looked at her, tearing his gaze away from her fabulous breasts.

"Back to my business. We think that Lawson Blaine was murdered. We don't believe the accident story. Do you have any idea who might have been behind his killing, or why? I know you talk to a lot of different men, including Judge Washington Maxwell. Could he have been behind it?"

Sally pushed him back on the bed and sat on his hips. She bent forward so her long red hair covered his face. He blew it aside.

"Sally, do you know who killed Lawson Blaine?"

"If I did, I couldn't tell you."

"Is Maxwell behind it?"

"If I knew, I couldn't say."

"Is J. D. Clatter one of the villains here?"

"If he is, I couldn't tell you."

She bent forward, lowering one of her breasts into his mouth. "At least I know one good way to stop you talking. Now, enjoy. Half the afternoon is gone already. I'm a working girl. I have to be pretty for the evening trade."

Ki moaned and chewed on her fine breasts. She was right; it would always be a fine way to keep him quiet. But somehow he had to find out what she knew. As he thought about it, he decided she had answered him already. She knew nothing about Lawson's death—most likely.

With that settled, Ki got both hands working and began to enjoy this amazing woman again. It would be a tough job for the rest of the afternoon, but he could handle it.

★

Chapter 7

Jessie left the widow Blaine's house knowing exactly what she wanted to do. This whole problem could turn out to be centered around the Ready Relief mine. She had to go back there and find out everything she could. This time she'd take a slightly different approach.

She slipped into her riding jeans, buckled on her gunbelt, with the .38 Colt in the leather, and hired a horse. She knew the way. Ki was busy, and there would be no real danger for her.

She rode quickly to the Ready Relief mine, five miles east from Julian proper, along the drop-off into the desert. She went past two buildings and tied her horse outside the office where she had talked to Maxwell before.

He came out of the building puffing on a pipe. When he first saw Jessie, he didn't recognize her. Then he nodded.

"Thought we had our talk out the other day," Maxwell said.

"Hello and good morning to you, Mr. Maxwell. I'm here on a far different errand this morning. I own some coal mines, but they're much different from this gold business. Frankly, I want you to show me something about gold mining, what happens once the ore gets to the surface."

"I'm not running a school for rich ladies, here, Miss Starbuck. But looks like I'll be worse than the rear end of a donkey unless I show you what we do here. How much of an understanding do you want?"

"Just enough to see if I think that it would a good idea for me to invest in a gold mine here in the Julian area. Most of these mines are highly underfinanced, from what I've been able to learn. An infusion of fresh money might make a big difference in their profit picture, but I don't know a lot about the crushing and smeltering aspect of gold mining."

Maxwell seemed to relax. "Guess you wondering about investing can't all be bad. Not that I'm looking for any part- ners, but there's a bunch of mine owners here in town who could damn well use some ready cash. Oh, pardon my lan- guage."

"No offense, Mr. Maxwell. I work around men all the time, and I've heard language that would make a sailor blush. Where do we begin?"

Maxwell stared at her sidearm. "You know how to use that thing?"

"If I need to. It's a .38 mated to a .44-caliber Colt frame. Works out well for me. First the ore comes out of the tunnels or up a hoist from a shaft; then what happens?"

They walked around a huge pile of worthless rock that had been hauled out from the mine.

"Lots of this around," Maxwell said. "You've got to move it out of the way to get to the white quartz veins that have the gold." They walked uphill a ways, and he pointed to a set of narrow steel rails coming out of a tunnel.

"Right now most of our ore comes from that tunnel. The cars come down the tracks. If they have ore in them, they go slightly downhill to the stamp mill. If it's just worthless schist, we switch it to that other track, and it all gets dumped at the end, down into the gully and out of the way.

"The ore cars go to the stamp mill. Chariot Creek usu- ally runs enough water here to power our stamp mill. We run two mills down there. That's what's making all of the noise."

"Can we go down and look at them?" Jessie asked.

62

"Can. It gets noisy down there, so let's talk some up here, first. The stamp mills are steel on steel. The ore is fed in as needed by gravity, and the stamps turn the quartz ore into a fine pulverized powder. Looks like coarse sand by the time it gets finished. It has to be fine enough to sift through screens that we have on each stamp mill."

"So the gold is still mixed in with the coarse sand?" Jessie asked.

"Right. Then that mixture is spread in the big flat pans just below the stampers you'll see down there and washed with a mixture of mercury and water. The mercury attracts the gold and picks it up. The sand and little rocks that got through the screen but contain no gold wash away into a trough and are collected so they can be processed again. We miss about ten percent of the gold when it goes through the stamp mill.

"Once a day we stop the stamping process and scrape the mercury and its gold off the big sloped trays. This product is called amalgam. This mixture of gold and mercury is put in special containers and taken under guard to our smeltering shed, where it's kept until we have enough to start up the smeltering process."

"Can we go down and look at the stamping? Sounds like a lot more work than just mining coal."

"But when we get through, we have a product that must be worth say a thousand times more than coal is worth."

Jessie nodded. "Good point."

They walked down a trail, toward the stamp mill below. Without warning, the big man stopped suddenly.

"Don't move," he said over his shoulder. "I just kicked a rock and it hit a big rattlesnake sunning himself in the path. Now he's coiled and looks mad as hell. He's about a foot from my ankle, and I don't have on my knee-high boots today."

Jessie drew her .38 Colt, leaned around the large man, and fired once. The triangular head of the Pacific diamondback rattler took the round just as its jaws opened to strike, and the blow shattered the serpent's skull over half a country mile and tore the snake's body off the trail, to lie twitching in death spasms.

Maxwell turned, his white face wreathed in surprise. A grin broke through. "Damn! Guess I don't have to ask again if you're any good with that little .38. Looks good enough for me." He shook his head. "I figured for damn sure I was gonna have myself at least one rattler bite. I've had them before and they're no fun. The bite swells up something fierce and gets hot and hurts like hell. One bite usually isn't enough to kill a man, but it's no church social hour either." He kicked the remains of the snake off the trail. "Let's get on down to the stamp mill."

They came at the mill from the side. The pair of stampers sat near the creek, where an overshot waterwheel created the power to run the mill.

Each of the devices stood ten feet tall and included a three-foot flywheel attached to a shaft that had five concentrics. Each time the shaft turned, the concentrics lifted the long steel hammer bars one at a time and then let each one fall in sequence. They smashed downward, with the big steel hammer on the bottom of each slamming into the ore that covered the steel bottom of the mill.

The noise came from the steel hammers battering the rock and quartz and gold into finer and finer particles. The banging of the two stampers side by side, each with its five hammers, made an earth shaking rumble in the ground and a din of noise as well.

Men worked letting more raw ore fall into the mill's maw when it was needed, making sure the crushed material was fine enough to sift through the screen and then directly below onto the six-by-four tray where the liquid mercury completed the amalgamation process.

"Here we're lucky," Maxwell shouted so Jessie could hear. "Almost no other metals—silver or lead or copper—are mixed in with the quartz, so all we need to separate the gold is the mercury. In other places they need several other chemicals to get to the gold, and it's a much harder and more expensive process."

They walked a distance away from the stamp mill so they could talk easier.

"You said the amalgam caught only ninety percent of the gold. What happens to the other ten percent?"

"The sand and gravel and dust that comes off the first table is transferred to another table that is constantly shaken. It's a kind of gold panning. The lighter material works off the end of the table, and the heavier gold particles stay in cleats on the table and are gathered and processed. This way we can save all but about two percent of the gold in our white quartz ore."

Jessie nodded, filing it all in her mind. She would be able to recall at least 90 percent of what they had talked about.

"Then when you have the amalgam, what happens with it? Isn't mercury poisonous?"

"The mercury vapor certainly is. Let me show you the smeltering shed."

Inside the shed, near the face of the mountain, Jessie saw a furnace, some equipment to move molten metal, and another device that looked like a still that she had seen once in the backwoods of Missouri.

"A still?" she asked.

"That mercury vapor is deadly. When we boil it off the amalgam and pour out the molten gold, the still collects the mercury vapor and condenses it in the tubes, where it turns into a harmless liquid, and we can reuse it for more amalgam."

The furnace was cold and the still silent.

"So this isn't a continuous process here in the smeltering shed?"

Maxwell laughed. "I wish it could be. We aren't that big an operation that we need to smelter our amalgam every day. If so, I would soon be a millionaire and could go live in San Francisco and never work another day in my life. We fire up our furnace here when we need to, depending how rich the vein is that we're working and how much amalgam we produce."

Jessie nodded as they walked out into the noontime sunshine.

"Looks like getting the gold ore out of the ground is only half the job," Jessie said. "The gold still must be separated from the quartz. With coal, when you get it to the surface, it's ready to ship or to burn."

They started back up the hill, toward the mine.

"Mr. Maxwell, I'm not sure that I want to get involved in gold mining after all. Underground is not my favorite place. On the other hand, I could hire good men to do the job for me."

They talked a few minutes more near Jessie's horse.

"Mr. Maxwell, I'm still concerned about Lawson Blaine's death. He was a dear friend who worked for me for six years in Texas. You've told me what happened and I appreciate it. Now I'm trying to help the widow. If any more details of Lawson's death come to light, I'd be glad if you sent me a note. I'm staying at the Julian Hotel."

Maxwell said he would send in anything new he discovered. Then he laced his fingers together to give her a step up to the stirrup of her horse and she lifted into the saddle.

"Please, Mr. Maxwell, the smallest detail may be important concerning Lawson's death. All the comfort we can give the widow will be that much more help for her. Thanks for the tour and the information about quartz gold. I'll have to decide later about investing here."

Jessie Starbuck turned and rode back the way she had come.

Judge Washington Maxwell had spotted the horse tied over near the mine when they first came up from the stamp mill. He thought he knew what it meant. Now he could find out for sure.

In the office, he met a man waiting patiently on a hard-backed chair.

The man was slender, dark, had a wind-toughened face and hands with rope and leather burns all over them. The two men went into Maxwell's office and sat down.

"The run will be tonight, Mr. Maxwell. I'll be driving the stage and we should get here about two A.M. if all goes well. You're the last stop; then we'll head for San Diego on the new route through Cuyamaca City and down past the lake."

"Fine, we'll be ready. I'll have five bricks all packed and set to go. You can have the manifest and guarantee all written up for me when you get here. That will speed things up."

"Good. I better be on my way, Mr. Maxwell. Looks like you're ahead of me this time. Near as I can tell, we'll have about fifteen bricks on this run."

The two men shook hands. No one else at the mine knew who the caller was or what would happen later that night. It was the mandatory procedure laid down by Wells Fargo.

They guaranteed the delivery of the gold into the hands of U.S. Treasury agents at the dock in San Diego, and they were taking no chances. All of the mine owners cooperated.

Maxwell waited until the man had ridden out, then he went out to the smeltering shed, waved at one of the two outside guards, and had him open the heavy oak door that led directly into the mountain, by way of a worked-out tunnel. Into the tunnel twenty feet, a "room" had been dug out. Now the room was used to store the amalgam and the finished gold bars. They were about four inches square and four inches high. Into the top of each one had been stamped the date it was poured and the special mark to identify the mine, two capital Rs that slightly overlapped at the bottom.

Maxwell counted the gold bricks lined up on a shelf set against the raw schist of the wall. Yes, five bricks. They weighed about ten pounds each. Gold was worth $20.37 per ounce, so each of the bars was valued at a little under $3,300. That was more than $16,000 worth of gold he would be sending. The whole shipment's worth would be almost $50,000.

Maxwell turned and motioned to the guard that he wanted to leave. He closed the inside door on the tunnel, then knocked on the outside door that led into the smeltering shed. The guard pulled it open, and Maxwell watched the man close it and stand in front of it. Then he went back to the office.

Yes, he would be ready. By two A.M. everything would be arranged quite neatly.

When Jessie got back to town, she put the horse in the livery and walked to Vince Hirlbach's office on Main Street. She pushed open the door and swept inside.

Vince looked up from some charts and graphs on his desk and grinned.

"How about lunch? I've been waiting for you to show up."

Jessie frowned. "You figured I'd be coming around?"

"Figured, hoped. Mostly hoped. I'd take you to the best restaurant in town, but there isn't one."

They both laughed. "How about the cafe three doors down? I haven't been poisoned there yet."

During the meal Vince told her what he'd found out by asking around.

"Not a lot, but looks like there could be a classic power struggle shaping up. Somebody wants to control all of the mines in the area. It's been tried before. It was called the great Cuyamaca land grant battle.

"An old Spanish land grant was first denied, then won back, and came into the hands of four men back in 1869. They bought it for the timber on the land, mostly north of town from what I hear.

"They got a title suit dismissed and asked the court for what their lawyer called a new boundary survey of their property. In the process these four new owners of the land grant 'floated' their boundary to include the entire Julian mining district, and all of the Julian mines.

"The land grant owners then demanded a royalty from the mine owners for all the ore they took out of their mines. What it amounted to was a fifty percent split of the profits on the gold. The mine owners refused the royalty. Most stopped work. Equipment orders were canceled.

"It went to a court battle. New mines were discovered, but none of the land under litigation could be bought or sold. Took four years of legal hassles before the mine owners finally won the court battle back in 1873."

"Let's hope nothing like that is shaping up here," Jessie said.

"Can't happen again. But what can happen is the usual pattern on a land grab like this: One big miner starts squeezing out the smaller ones. There might be accidents, explosions, trouble among the workers, that sort of thing that would wear down an owner to the point where he would be glad to sell at a reduced price. Then the vulture sweeps in, grabs the mine, and goes to work on the next victim."

"Clatter behind it?"

"Not saying it's happening here, but there are some of the usual pressures. Could be Clatter, could be Maxwell, or half a dozen other mine owners. Clatter is a master at such tactics. He's a lawyer as well, which makes it easier for him. Legal shenanigans are how he won the mine he owns now. Clatter had me do a secret evaluation of two neighboring mines."

They finished their meal and over coffee talked about Texas. Vince had been through it several times, but it wasn't a big mining state.

When their coffee was gone, he looked at Jessie. "Could I take you to dinner tonight? Then we'll go to the Julian Town Hall and see the Variety show out of Chicago."

Jessie laughed softly. "Sounds nice, but Julian doesn't have a theater or a town hall, and there isn't any variety show. Outside of that, dinner sounds like fun. Do you play poker?"

"Love the game. I'll pick you up at your room in the hotel at about six."

They went their separate ways outside the cafe. Jessie marched down to the town marshal's office and stepped inside.

Myles Zane looked up from his checkerboard. He grumbled deep in his throat, not any words, more like a groan.

"Yeah? What do you want?"

"Good afternoon to you, too, Marshal Zane. I just wondered if you had any wanted posters from Wyoming?"

"Now, why in the . . ." He looked over at his checker opponent, who shook his head at the marshal. "Why would I have any wanted posters from Wyoming? This here is California. Even a woman from Texas should be able to tell the difference."

"No wanteds at all from Wyoming?"

"Right, lady. I got no wanted posters at all from anywhere. They all go to the county sheriff down in San Diego. You ride down there and ask him your question, and he'll more than likely have an answer for you. He usually does. Have an answer. For everyone about anything. That all?"

"Yes, Marshal, that's all. You get back to your checker game. If you don't make it to the king row in three moves, your chances of winning that game are next to nothing." Jessie saw the surprised look on the lawman's face as she walked out the front door.

Jessie strolled down the boardwalk. She had no idea what to do next. Had she come to the end of the line on this killing? She was sure it was a murder. All she had to do was prove it.

She saw a woman's wear store across the street and challanged a buggy and a freight wagon by hiking across and making it through the half inch of dust to reach the boardwalk.

The store was a combination ready-to-wear and seamstress shop. Jessie opened the door and hurried inside before she could change her mind. A new blouse, no, two new blouses; she could do with a few. How long had it been?

A woman looked up from a sewing machine. She had pins in her mouth, so she nodded and waved. A moment later the sewing machine treadle went silent, and the woman took the pins out of her mouth.

"Afternoon, Miss. I'm Hattie. What can I do for you today?"

Jessie headed for a rack of bright colored blouses and hoped that there was something there her size. If there wasn't, she'd have the seamstress cut something down for her. The afternoon was starting to look brighter already.

"I'm looking for a new blouse or two." For dinner that night with Vince she could wear her traveling skirt, a new blouse, and maybe a kerchief in a contrasting color. Jessie smiled to herself. Tonight was for her. Tomorrow she'd worry again about what happened to Lawson Blaine.

★
Chapter 8

Late that same night, the Wells Fargo gold wagon pulled to a stop outside of the office at the Ready Relief. It was a standard coach, one of the big Concords that had served the trails west so well before the train tracks went coast to coast. The driver jumped down and knocked on the office door. A moment later it opened.

"Wells Fargo," the driver said. "I'm Pat Nathan. I was here earlier to give you the schedule."

Washington Maxwell stared at the man until he was sure it was the same one who had been there to notify him of the gold run. He grunted.

"Yeah, come in, Nathan. I got five gold bricks for you. Put them in a special wooden box to hold them. Stow it with the others. I'll help you carry it out. Had a man put rope handles on each end."

They carried the heavy, narrow box from the office and pushed it through the door of the big Concord coach. Two men in the shadows inside the coach took the gold and put it in a special metal box. They slammed the cover on and twisted handles to seal the steel chest.

"Got that thing bolted to the floor?" Maxwell asked.

Pat Nathan nodded. "Yep. Took out the center seat and

bolted this strongbox in its place. That way she's centered and secure."

He closed the stage door. "We always use a regular coach so nobody knows that there's anything special about the run. Just doing it at night. It's worked so far. I better be getting down the south road."

"You take care of my goods there, Nathan. I got more than sixteen thousand dollars' worth of U.S. greenbacks in that little box of gold."

"We'll take good care. Ain't lost none yet; don't aim to." Nathan stepped up to the high seat, unwound the reins of the six horses, and turned the rig around. He gave one last wave and then angled the team out the dark trail back to Julian and the south road, which would take him past Lake Cuyamaca and on down the grades to the community of Alpine and into the east side of San Diego. It was the most direct route, the newest, and the road that had the most mountains on it.

A little more than an hour later, the Concord slowed to go down a steep grade south of Julian. Pat Nathan pulled back the lead team and pushed on the foot brake that brought a wooden block hard against the front stage wheel. He got the rig slowed to his usual speed, an easy walk down this narrow and steep road along the side of the bluff, and stared ahead in the darkness.

He knew this road better at night than in the day. A half moon cast a host of ghost figures across the slender trail ahead. For just a moment Nathan felt a pang of fear; then he snorted and eased the horses along past the steepest drop-off along the whole route. His lead horses knew the trail better than he did. He had complete confidence in them.

Without warning, a rifle shot snarled in the mountain-high quiet, and one of the lead horses staggered and fell. On top of the first shot came three more. One killed the second lead horse, and it fell toward the emptiness to the right side of the coach.

Before Pat Nathan could do more than jerk backward on the reins, two shotguns blasted double-ought buck rounds from a clump of pines twenty feet away. Half of the twenty-four .32-caliber balls in the two shotgun rounds hit Nathan, two in the head, four in the chest. The rounds blew him off the high

72

seat, spun him over the side of the coach, and dumped him into the hundred-foot void. Below lay only a jumble of rock blasted out of the side of the mountain to form the road.

The lead horse careened sideways. The second team followed, and a moment later the six animals fell or were dragged off the road, pulling the Concord coach with them as the lash-up plunged through empty space to the deadly consequences of a sudden stop on the rocks far below.

Down at the crash site, one of the horses bleated in terror and pain. A man's voice called with a weak plea for help from far below.

Across the road three men stood from their concealed positions and walked to the lip of the chasm to look down.

"We did it damn good!" one of the men holding a shotgun said.

The taller of the three nodded. "Now let's get the horses down there and take what we came for."

The three vanished into the brush and returned to the road a few minutes later. They rode three hundred yards down the steep grade, to a point where their horses could work across the sloping bank to the canyon below.

Once on the bottom, they moved back up the gully toward the site of the crash. One horse still screamed in agony. When they had worked their way to the smashed coach and the horses, one of the men swore.

"Christ, what a mess!"

"Kill that wounded horse," the tallest man said.

"Help me." A feeble cry came from the coach wreckage. The Concord had lost all four wheels; the top had been hit first, and the body of the rig was crushed nearly flat.

The tall man rushed up to the wreckage, searching for the man who was still alive.

"Where are you?" the bushwhacker called.

"Here, here. Pinned in." The voice, which was probably that of one of the guards inside the coach, came fainter now.

The big man swung part of the broken wreckage aside and found the injured driver. A moment later his six-gun boomed in the tall timber silence, and the wounded man cried out no more.

73

"Good God!" one of the robbers whispered. The other one shrugged.

"Get the gold," the tall man barked.

They found the strongbox broken open. Even in the faint moonlight they could see the gold bricks lying in the rubble. Ten of them were nearby. They had to light a torch to find the rest of them scattered in the grass and weeds; two of the bricks lay under some of the wreckage.

They loaded two of the bricks in each side of their saddlebags. That made twelve. Then the tall man unrolled a gunnysack, put the last four gold bars into it, and tied it to his saddle horn.

"Let's get out of here," he said. He rode faster now, back down the gully, up to the road, and along the trail south for two miles, before he turned off with the other two riders and took a little-used trail back into a wooded valley.

"Old miner's cabin back in here," the tall man said. "He built a good cabin but never did strike his vein. Gave it up ten years ago."

They found the log house after two tries. It was up the third little canyon branching off the main valley.

"Place ain't been used in years, but it'll do for tonight," the leader said. "We'll stay here the rest of the night. We continue on down trail in the morning and get out of the way of anyone riding north. Get your blankets and we'll go inside."

As soon as the men had their blankets off the horses and their arms full of gear, they turned toward the man who had hired them.

"Payoff time, gentlemen," the tall man said. He shot the first man with a six-gun round in the heart and hit the second one as he tried to draw. The second man went down with one round in his chest and a final round through his left ear and into the top of his head.

The tall man stared at the two bodies a moment. "Men, don't never trust nobody, not with fifty thousand dollars involved." He snorted, then took a shovel from the side of the cabin, where he had left it a week before. He dragged the bodies away from the cabin door.

It took him two hours to dig a hole deep enough to get a foot of dirt over the pair. Then he put the dead men's saddlebags on one horse, tied on the gunnysack with the last four bricks of gold, and led the two animals behind him as he moved out toward the main road to Julian.

Once he hit the wagon road, he untied the third horse and left it hitched to a tree, then picked up the pace. He'd have to rush now to get back to Julian before daylight. The closer to dawn, the better, though, because then there would be more traffic on the road and streets to cover his own trail.

The tall man patted his saddlebags as he rode. Not a bad night's work. He had fifty thousand dollars in gold, and none of the mine owners would lose a dollar, because Wells Fargo would make good on their contract to reimburse any loss. Yes, a damn fine night's work.

Early the next morning, Jessica came down the hotel stairs from the second floor to the lobby at a leisurely pace. It had been an interesting evening with Vince. They had had a long dinner, then a walk along the street and an hour's conversation in the two chairs at the back of the lobby. Vince was much more than he seemed on the surface. He was articulate, well read, finely educated, and more attractive than she wanted to admit even to herself. Perhaps when she had the time . . .

As Jessie came down the last flight of steps into the lobby and turned toward the dining room, a man rose from a chair facing the stairs and approached her.

"Miss Starbuck?" His voice was calm, even, and he wore a business suit with vest and gold chain. She paused. She had never seen him before.

"Yes, I'm Jessica Starbuck."

"Good. I gambled that the most beautiful lady in the hotel this morning would have to be you. We've never met. My name is J. Downing Clatter. I'm an attorney here in town and also happen to own one of Julian's gold mines. Would you permit me to invite you to breakfast?"

She hesitated. She had heard of this man, wondered about him. It might be a way to smoke him out.

"As it happens, I know the Starbuck name," Clatter said. "Your father, Alex Starbuck, is still a legend in the importing business. I studied his operation in one of my classes at law school. Amazing. I've been through Texas and know about the Circle Star ranch out in the west part of the state, but I've never been there. I'd be honored if you'd let me show you the hospitality that our quaint little city here hasn't done so far."

Jessie nodded. "Yes, I'd be pleased to accept your invitation. But I'm warning you, I eat breakfast like I was on a roundup."

"That great. I'm a big eater myself. They have a miner's breakfast here that should take care of your needs." He took her arm and piloted her into the dining room. The headwaiter nodded to them and showed them to a special table near the window, where they could see the high ridges beyond town.

Clatter seated Jessica, then sat directly across from her. Without asking her, he ordered a pot of coffee and two cups, then the Big Miner's Special breakfast for both of them. A waiter returned quickly with the coffee, and they both sampled it.

"Miss Starbuck, I know that you're in town on personal business, but I hope while you're here, I can show you some mining property that soon will be up for sale. I want to buy it, but I need a partner. That means I'm a little short of cash."

He held up his hand as she started to reply.

"I know, I know, you aren't too thrilled about all of the work it takes after gold ore gets brought to the surface. It isn't like coal mining and I understand that. Still, I'd like the chance to talk to you about the benefits of all that stamping and smeltering work."

"I'm here on a private and personal matter, Mr. Clatter. However, I'm always interested in learning about new things. Yesterday I had a tour of the stamping and amalgam works out at the Ready Relief."

"So I heard. Maxwell has a good operation going there. Did you know there are twenty-four mines in the Julian and Banner Grade area? Not all of them are producing right now, but most of them have a great potential."

"How did you get into the mine-owning business, Mr. Clatter?"

"By chance, I'm afraid, Miss Starbuck. I took a mine owner as a legal client, and one thing led to another, and a run-down mine that didn't produce enough gold to pay its expenses became payment for my legal fees. I'm not altogether pleased with the situation, but it's a challenge, I can tell you that."

Clatter was not at all what Jessie had expected. He was medium size, maybe five feet ten, slender, and not over thirty-five. He had dark wavy hair and a rather stern face that could break into a smile at the hint of something humorous.

She saw little evidence that he could be behind any large-scale plot to take over all of the Julian mines. Still he was a lawyer, and she had never been overly trusting of legal experts.

"Perhaps you'd like to take a tour underground on the High Peak mine. That's the one I own. I have a worked-out tunnel that would show you what goes on down there—" He stopped when Jessie held up one hand.

"I really don't have the time, Mr. Clatter. I appreciate your offer, but today is shaping up to be a busy one for me. Besides, I much prefer the clear mountain air to that in some stuffy old mine tunnel."

Their breakfast came then. Jessie saw why Clatter had ordered it. The meal was huge. A six-high pancake stack held down the center of the plate. Each flapjack was half an inch thick and eight inches across. On one side lay a stack of bacon, and on the other side slices of sausage. Three fried eggs scalloped the front of the plate. Then the waiter brought four slices of toast, two kinds of jam, fresh butter, and another pot of coffee.

Clatter grinned as Jessie looked up from the meal big enough to stuff a lumberjack.

"Now, this is a breakfast. Nothing like this around my bachelor house, so I often take my morning nourishment down here."

Twenty minutes passed before either of them said much more. They both spent the time eating.

At last Jessie pushed back and sighed. "I don't think that I'm going to want any lunch today. You're right. That's a lot of breakfast." She looked up at Clatter and decided to probe. "Now that you have one mine, Mr. Clatter, are you really in the market for more, or was that just an opening gambit?"

"I'm not that much of a chess player, Miss Starbuck. Yes,

I'd love to own half the producing mines in the Julian mining district, but I don't have the capital or the energy to own and manage them."

"At least you're honest about it. Could I ask you another question?"

"By all means." His smile would have charmed a cattle rustler into giving up his long rope.

"Do you know anything about how or why Lawson Blaine died out at the Ready Relief?"

Clatter scrubbed one hand over his face and frowned. "You're direct, aren't you, Miss Starbuck? But then I expect with your wealth and position, you can afford to be. The fact is I heard that it was an ore-car crash. That's all I know. There have been no rumors or suggestion that it was anything but an accident. I understand that you think he was murdered."

"Yes. Lawson Blaine was not a careless man. He would no more get caught between two ore cars than he would shoot off his right foot."

The mine owner shook his head. "I'm sorry I can't help you. This is not from any loyalty to Washington Maxwell. Don't be fooled by that 'Judge' he tacks on the start of his name. He was named a justice of the peace for six months in some little town back in Ohio and has traded on that fact ever since. I'm not a friend of Mr. Maxwell's, but I have no reason to suspect any foul play in the death of your friend."

"Did the sheriff investigate?"

"No. Don't think he's been in Julian since he was elected over three years ago. He'll come up and campaign for votes, but that's about the only time we see him. Mining is dangerous work. A man gets killed in and around these mines every so often. Something like twenty men have died in mining accidents here in Julian the last few years."

"So everyone gets used to it, insulated from the deaths?"

"Something like that."

The breakfast had stretched out, and Jessie saw by the clock near the entrance that it was almost nine.

"I really should be going. Thank you for the fine breakfast. You were right. I didn't quite get it all finished."

Clatter smiled. "Neither did I. Could I see you to somewhere in town? Your first appointment?"

"No, but thank you. I need to go back to my room to get some material. It's been interesting meeting you. If I decide to look at any mining property here, you'll be the first one I come to."

He stood and helped move back her chair, and they walked out of the dining room. They parted at the stairs, and Jessie went back to her room. She had on a town skirt and one of her new blouses, but that didn't seem right for today. She changed into her riding clothes and her low-crowned brown Stetson with the flat brim. She looked at her gunbelt over the chair and decided not this time.

She double-checked the two-shot derringer in her reticule, locked her door, and hurried down to Ki's room. Nobody answered her knock on his door. He might be in the dining room. A quick check there proved he wasn't having breakfast.

Jessie had just started down the outside steps of the hotel when Ki came up from the street.

"Missed you at breakfast," Ki said. "Had mine early. I haven't turned up anything new or valuable. What about talking to some of Lawson's friends around town?"

"I found out about one yesterday. We can track him down today. Agatha told me where he lives."

They had started down the boardwalk when a rider came into town from the south trail. His lathered mount strained to complete the ride. The young man on the back of the bay had lost his hat, and his eyes were wide as he raced up to the Wells Fargo office.

"The stage, the gold wagon stage," he bellowed as he jumped off his horse. "Somebody slaughtered the driver and two guards, killed the horses, and stole all of the gold!"

★

Chapter 9

Two hours after the rider thundered into town, Jessie, Ki, and about twenty other riders arrived at the death scene. The town marshal was not among them; out of his jurisdiction, he had told one angry mine owner.

The men dug into the crash and brought out the two dead guards. Ki saw the bullet wound in the man's chest but said nothing. When they found the last man it was plain to see he had been shotgunned.

"Damn bad," the Wells Fargo agent from Julian said. "Somebody is gonna pay for this. The bastards killed three good men."

By the time Ki and Jessie had worked down to the crash scene, there had been a dozen horses up and down the canyon.

"Any tracks that were here are gone by now," Ki said. He checked for the prints of a heavily laden horse but couldn't make out any.

At last he and Jessie went back up to the road and searched the area just across from the crash. They found the place where the rig had gone off the road and checked the brush on the far side, away from the drop-off.

Jessie picked up two empty shotgun shells. Ki discovered

where a man had spent some time—smoked three cigarettes and stubbed them out—and nearby he came across four copper casings from rifle rounds.

"They gunned them from here, but where did the killers go after they stole the gold?" Jessie asked.

They checked the road downhill first, since it had been less traveled. To their surprise they found prints of three horses, and all of them looked a little heavier than usual. The three had had no special marks on their shoes.

There had been little traffic down the road this early in the day, and they followed the prints for two miles, then turned off and angled along a little-used trail.

"Probably an old mining road," Jessie said. The tracks were confused at the first and second small valleys that led off the trail, but at the third one they found clear prints heading up a little creek.

When they came to the cabin, they found more tracks. Then Ki called to Jessie.

"Look at this," he said, kneeling on the ground. Dark stains showed in the scattering of oak leaves and pine needles. "Blood," Ki said. He stood and searched the area close by. He walked away from the cabin, following what looked to Jessie like marks made when something had been dragged.

"The bodies?" Jessie asked.

"One or two, I'd guess," Ki said. "A cheap payoff for a killer or two."

Less than a hundred feet from the cabin, Ki found where fresh dirt had been turned. Leaves and pine needles had been brought to the area and scattered over the dirt, but he could see that it was newly worked. He took a stick and dug into the soft soil.

Five minutes later he hit something, and soon he unearthed the arm of a human body. Moments later he discovered the second body under the first.

Jessie shook her head. "Three men slaughter the gold wagon crew, then one of the three kills the other two and takes off with all the gold. I wonder how much was on that rig."

"We can find out from Wells Fargo," Ki said.

"Any chance we can track the horses out of here?" Jessie

asked. "All three must have been taken away."

Ki worked for half an hour and at last pinpointed three sets of tracks leaving the cabin. One set was normal, but the other two were faint.

"No riders on two of the mounts," he said.

They lost them twice, but worked ahead and found the tracks again as they came to the road. Ki noticed a place across the stage road where one horse had spent some time. There were droppings and wet spots on the ground.

It took him a half hour to pick up the trail of two horses that had taken the road back north toward Julian. One showed normal horseshoe prints; the other set was light.

By the time they came to the wreck scene, they'd lost the tracks of the two horses in the maze of prints from all those horses that had been ridden out to the scene.

The crash area was deserted. Two riders still sat their mounts on the road above and looked down. Jessie didn't know either of them.

"They took the three bodies back to Julian," one of the strangers said. "It was the Wells Fargo man who did it. No law out this way. Damned shame the sheriff don't get up here now and then."

Jessie and Ki agreed, then rode for Julian.

"Just before we lost the tracks, I took a closer look at them," Ki said. "They were made during the night sometime. Both sets had insect tracks across them, night critters that come out to feed after dark. The tracks made by our horses this morning have no marks of any kind made by the little creatures."

"So the killer took the gold back toward Julian last night or just before dawn," Jessie said.

"Looks that way. Means anyone in Julian could have done the killing."

Jessie shook her head. "Vince told me how the gold wagon works. Not even the mine owners know when it's going to come until the afternoon of the run. Somebody from Wells Fargo tells the mine owners they'll be past just after midnight."

"So any robber would have to watch the mines after midnight and hope to get lucky, or be one of the men at the mines who knows the gold is being shipped," Ki said.

"Vince said that usually only the mine owner or manager is told that the gold is going. So they know, and any of the men who see it loaded. That cuts down the suspects."

"Do you think this ties in with Lawson's death?"

Jessie turned her horse over to the stable man at the livery in Julian and nodded. "Looks like the one and only good reason we have for Lawson being killed. At least that's something big enough to get a man murdered—if he knew about a planned robbery like this."

"Say there was ten thousand dollars in gold on the wagon. That's more than a miner makes in fifteen or sixteen years. Quite an incentive for robbery and murder."

"Or it could have been a mine owner," Jessie suggested. "Fifteen or twenty of them would know about the run, even those who didn't have any gold to ship."

"Steal from themselves?" Ki asked.

"Wells Fargo guarantees every gold shipment. Steal from yourself and get it back from Wells Fargo. You're ahead twice on your own shipment."

They walked toward the hotel. They had missed lunch, but Jessie wasn't hungry after that huge breakfast.

"Let's see if we can find Lawson's best friend. His name is Earl Frenken, and he's supposed to live on C Street somewhere."

They had to ask at two houses; then they found the one where the Frenkens lived. Ki knocked on the front door.

A short woman carrying a baby, and with a small girl clinging to her legs, opened the door.

"Is this where Earl Frenken lives?" Jessie asked.

"Right. Who are you?"

"I'm Jessie Starbuck, and I was a good friend of Lawson Blaine's. I understand your husband was one of his best friends."

"Don't know. Earl don't talk much. He's on the day shift out at the Ready Relief. Be home about six tonight if'n you want to talk with him."

83

"Thank you, Mrs. Frenken. I'll come back later on tonight."

They trudged down the slope, toward Main Street. Jessie told Ki about the wanted poster Lawson had mentioned to his wife.

"Rock Springs," Jessie said. "I used to know the deputy sheriff there. Let's send a wire to him and see if he can remember who Lawson was interested in. It just might produce a suspect we can get a noose around."

They went to the telegraph office. The wires had been strung up the Banner Grade about three years ago. They went down into the desert and then followed the old Overland Stage route into San Diego.

Jessie wrote out the wire, checked it, made some changes, and then gave it to the key man. The wire read:

"DEPUTY SHERIFF, ROCK SPRINGS, WYOMING. LAWSON BLAINE FROM JULIAN, CALIFORNIA, RECENTLY REQUESTED INFORMATION FROM YOU ABOUT A WANTED POSTER. DO YOU REMEMBER WHO THE WANTED MAN WAS? BLAINE MURDERED HERE. HUNTING SUSPECTS. IF YOU HAVE A DUPLICATE COPY, PLEASE SEND POSTER TO ME BY MAIL GENERAL DELIVERY, JULIAN. ALSO SEND BY RETURN WIRE THE NAME AND DESCRIPTION OF THE WANTED MAN. JESSICA STARBUCK."

She paid the fee from her reticule, and they went back to Main Street.

Jessie had told Ki about her early morning session with J. D. Clatter.

"He still sounds wrong somehow to me," Ki said. "Maybe I should follow him for the rest of the day and see what he does. He didn't buy you breakfast just to pass the time of day."

"I had the idea he was testing me, checking me out to see what else I was doing in town besides looking for a killer. Do you think he was involved with the gold robbery?"

"He knew the wagon would be going to San Diego last night, since he's a mine owner," Ki said.

"So did fifteen or twenty other men."

"One of them killed the driver and the guards."

84

"And stole all the gold, but which one?"

"Right now I wouldn't count out J. Downing Clatter. He's either in his office or at the High Peak mine. I just might turn up something interesting."

"I'll check around town," Jessie said. "Lawson must have had more than one good friend. First I'm going to go see the gunsmith. Lawson was a nut about his firearms. Chances are he saw the gunsmith down a block there more than once while he was in town."

Ki nodded and turned back toward the office with J. D. Clatter's name on the door. He walked past the place once and through one unshuttered window saw no one inside. The second time past the office, he tried the door and found it to be locked.

It took him nearly a half hour to find the Eagle mine, about a mile west of Julian, and then due east of that he located the High Peak mine. Ki moved through what was left of the light brush near the mine and settled in some concealment to watch.

Workers moved in and out of the tunnel. Some carried Cousin Jack hammers, some long steel rods. Twice while he watched, ore cars came out of the tunnel and were unlatched and dumped on a worthless rock heap down a small canyon.

To one side he saw a square building that he figured must be the mine office. There was some printing on a board over the door, but Ki was too far away to make it out. One man from the mine tunnel went inside the building, and a moment later a man in a suit and vest came out. He pulled a watch from his vest pocket and checked the time. The two talked for a moment; then the man in the suit returned to the office.

Five minutes later the same man came out of the mine office and headed for town. This had to be Clatter. He looked as Jessie had described him. Where was he bound for? Ki checked the sun. It was no more than three in the afternoon, if that late.

Ki kept to whatever cover he could manage and followed Clatter toward town. He didn't go all the way to Main. He turned south on B Street and stopped at a house that Jessie had described. It had to be Agatha Blaine's house. Clatter walked casually past the place, then turned down the alley. He checked behind him, and when he saw no one watching, he strode to the rear porch door and, without knocking, entered the Blaine residence.

Ki lifted his dark brows. Now, there was a good reason to kill a man—to get his wife. He had to be sure. He settled down behind some lilac bushes, from where he could see both the front and back doors of the Blaine house, and waited.

Soon smoke came from the chimney. It was time to start supper. Agatha must have been cooking for two that night. There was no chance that Ki could get close enough to see in a window until after dark. He relaxed and watched. The smoke intensified, then nearly died out. A half hour later the smoke came again, evidently as new fuel revitalized the flames.

By five o'clock, darkness had closed around Julian. No one had come to or left the Blaine house. Ki checked the surrounding area and worked out his route to the side of the house, and when he had decided it was dark enough, he moved.

There were two houses between there and town, but only one on this side. Lights came on in all four houses, including the Blaines'. Ki slipped up to the back window and looked inside. A thin curtain covered the window, but it was the transparent kind. The room was a back bedroom, evidently used for storage.

Ki moved to the other side of the house, and from there he could see into the kitchen. J. D. Clatter sat at the table sipping from a bottle of beer. Agatha worked at the stove.

Clatter came away from the table and slipped up behind Agatha, pushing his body close against hers, his hands going around her and cupping her breasts.

She turned and smiled and said something. He spun her around and kissed her lips, then scooped her up and carried her out of the kitchen, through a door on the side of the house where Ki watched.

A new lamp glowed, in the next room, as Ki peered in the window. It was partly open, and the curtain wasn't designed to block the view.

Clatter bent over Agatha Blaine, who lay on the bed. Her skirt billowed around her waist, and her bare legs spread wide apart. Expertly Clatter opened the top of her dress until her breasts came free.

86

He moaned in anticipation.

"Aggie, how can you be so damn sexy and marvelous?" Clatter asked in a hoarse, needful voice. She reached up and kissed him and then pulled him down to lie on top of her.

Ki eased away from the window and marched back toward town. Yes, confirmed. Now Clatter became a much better candidate for killing Lawson Blaine. For the love of a woman like Agatha Blaine, some men would do anything.

How could Clatter have killed Lawson at another mine? Not hard. It could have been done at night, when few workers were above ground. Clatter could have surprised Lawson, shot or stabbed him, and left the body for Maxwell to find and figure out how to cover up. An accident always could be explained away. That might just have been what happened.

Ki hurried back to the hotel and checked at the dining room, but Jessie wasn't there. He found her hotel key still in her box at the clerk's desk. She must have been having supper at another cafe.

After checking four eateries in the small town, Ki hadn't found Jessie. He stopped at the last one and had dinner. Jessie would turn up. He wasn't worried about her. She could take care of herself. He was anxious to tell her what he had learned about Clatter and Agatha. For now, that would have to wait.

Ki put aside the problem and concentrated on enjoying his supper. He hadn't eaten since breakfast, and the steak had been cooked exactly to his taste.

★

Chapter 10

Early that same afternoon, when Jessie left Ki, she had gone to see the gunsmith. He was the only one in town and also worked on watches and clocks. His small shop crowded both items together in what looked like a confused mishmash, but Jessie had seen people like him before. He probably could find any particular item in about twenty seconds.

The name on the door was Fenton Glover. Jessie walked over to where a small man with a balding head and an eyepiece examined a pocket watch. She guessed he was about fifty. He was a little heavy and had a stubble that proved he hadn't shaved for two or three days. His long, slender fingers looked exactly right for delicate work on a fine timepiece or an expensive revolver.

"Mr. Glover?"

He looked up and dropped the eyepiece, catching it neatly in his hand.

"Oh, didn't hear you come in. The old ears ain't what they used to be. Yep, I'm Glover. What can I do for you today, pretty lady?"

"Well, thank you. I'm looking for some information."

He nodded. "You're the nice lady from Texas worried about how Lawson Blaine died. Figured you'd be around. Not a chance to keep something like that a secret in a town this small. We kind of like to know everybody else's business but not let anybody know our own.

"Yep, I knew Lawson. Good man. Pardon the expression, but he was a damn good man."

"I agree with you. He used to work on my ranch in Texas. I'm Jessica Starbuck, and I think Lawson was murdered. What have you decided?"

"Lawson came in from time to time. He was trying to buy an old dueling pistol I have. Really didn't want to sell it. He'd look at it, clean it, oil it up, then make me an offer. Five or six times he did that. Each time I turned him down."

The gunsmith stared out the front window of his shop. "Not a chance that Lawson died like they said he did. But how to prove it? Some of these mine owners think they're gods, do anything they want to.

"Last time Lawson was in, he said he would be able to make me a better offer on the pistol soon. Hinted that he was going to come into a big chunk of money right soon. He didn't say how, and I didn't ask. Not the sort of question one man asks another, especially when he's holding a dueling pistol."

Glover chuckled. He sobered and shook his head. "No sir, not a chance Lawson Blaine died between two ore cars. I figured that was a good way to cover up the real way he died. Smash up the body some, and a bullet hole wouldn't show none a'tall."

Jessie held out her hand. "Mr. Glover, I want to thank you for telling me what you think. Of course, as you say, proving just how Lawson died is the big problem. Now I'm more sure than ever that he was killed. Did he have any enemies in town who were so angry they would murder him?"

"Lawson? No, ma'am. Not at all. Far as I knew, everybody who met Lawson Blaine liked the man. Rotten shame he ain't with us no more. Besides, I probably would have sold that dueling pistol if Lawson had kicked up his offer by even fifteen dollars. I don't need the blamed thing, and nobody else around here appreciates a fine weapon like that."

Jessie thanked the gunsmith again and left the shop. Where now? She frowned thinking about it. She worked the far side of the street and talked with the hardware man, the blacksmith, and the gent who ran the livery. None of them had much to say about Lawson. Two of them said they knew him by sight, but had not known him that well.

Jessie strolled down the boardwalk, in no rush to get anywhere. She knew she should go back and see Lawson's good friend, but she couldn't do that until after dinner. She sensed someone come up behind her, and before she could turn around, a deep voice spoke.

"Don't look back, but someone is following you," a man said.

Jessie whirled, her hand darting for her reticule, but before she could draw the derringer, she recognized the grinning face of Vince Hirlbach.

"Don't shoot me down on Main Street," Vince said, throwing up his hands in a token defense, but his voice told her that he was speaking only partly in jest.

Jessie relaxed and took her hand out of her purse. "Not a good idea to sneak up on a lady that way, Vince."

He shook his head in wonder. "Your hand got in that reticule so fast. Glad I wasn't trying to do you any harm."

"I'm glad, too. It would have upset my whole afternoon if I'd shot you dead." Jessie's stern expression dissolved into a grin; then she laughed. "Just fooling you, engineer. I wouldn't really have shot you. However, after your dastardly deed, you can make amends by taking me for some coffee and giving me some advice."

"How about coffee, the advice, and some ice cream? The cafe down on the corner made some today and keeps it frozen between blocks of ice. Interested?"

Ten minutes later they worked on the strawberry ice cream and small cookies at the cafe. Jessie told Vince she was making a little progress and asked him if he had any new ideas on her problem.

"What about the gold robbery?" Vince asked. "Do you think it's tied in to Lawson's death? He worked in the smeltering shed, where he was around the gold bars, and then there's a gold robbery. About as close as I can tie it in. It could mean something, then again. . . ."

Jessie admitted that she had considered the idea. "There certainly would have been strong enough motive to kill a man who happened to overhear plans to rob all that virgin gold. But, again, we don't have even the suggestion of a small particle of proof."

They talked for another fifteen minutes. Then Vince said he had an appointment. "I have to leave now, but I do want to take you to dinner. Make up for sneaking up on you. Can I meet you about six in the hotel lobby?"

Jessie said she'd like that.

For the next three hours she walked Main Street. At ten stores she asked if the owners knew Lawson Blaine and if they wondered about how he died.

None of them had anything new. Not even the postmistress in the Julian General Store could help. Jessie went back to the hotel, had a bath, and changed into one of her new blouses and the soft matching skirt. She wanted clothes a little more ladylike for a dinner out.

They went to the Julian Cafe, the only place in town where Jessie hadn't eaten. It was small, homey, and the owner and cook came and took their order. He had only two items on the menu tonight: venison steak or a slab of prime rib. They both ordered the venison. The meat was fresh and cooked exactly right. Most people, Jessie thought, overcooked deer meat.

After dinner they walked slowly back toward the hotel. Jessie held Vince's arm.

"In polite society, it's not considered proper conduct for a lady to invite a gentleman to her hotel room," she said.

Vince looked down, a touch of surprise showing on his handsome face.

"That's in polite society, you say?"

"Yes, absolutely. Julian is, of course, a hotbed of polite society. The most proper ladies of Julian would be shocked at the least if I invited you up to my room."

"Oh, I quite agree. Shocking. However, for me it would be exciting, interesting, wonderful. Yes, shocking for the polite society ladies, but not for me."

"That's why I'm not going to invite you to my room." Jessie paused and tightened her grip on his arm. "You did mention that you have a small house you rent. If you were a true gentleman, you might invite me to see your home and maybe offer me a cup of tea."

Vince slowed their walk and stopped. He looked down at her and smiled. "In that case, we're going the wrong direction. I would be more than pleased, Miss Starbuck, if you would do me the honor of dropping in at my home for a few minutes. We might play some whist, or gin or even dominoes. Also I do have some tea."

Jessie smiled at him. She felt her blood racing. She wanted to reach up and kiss this man.

"Mr. Hirlbach, I'd be delighted to accept your kind invitation, even if the card games don't interest me. I would like to see your house."

They walked back half a block on Main, then turned up B Street and went to the next row of houses, where they turned left and walked down half a block to a small white bungalow that had an overlook of most of the town. Vince escorted Jessie to the door and ushered her inside.

He closed the door and, in the shadows, struck a match to light a closely placed lamp. Next he pulled down the roller shades on the windows, then lit another lamp.

They were in a living room, furnished in a utilitarian manner.

"I rent it as is," Vince said.

Jessie caught his hand and stepped close to him. She lifted her face toward him and with one hand around the back of his neck gently pulled his lips down to hers.

Jessie shivered as they kissed. The first kiss was soft and brief; the next was longer, and her arms went around him. She clung to him, pressing tightly.

When their lips eased apart, she sighed. "Oh my, but that is nice," Jessie said, looking up at him. "Vince, now and again I find a man I'm attracted to. I don't see anything wrong with letting him know about it. Does that surprise you?"

"Nothing about you surprises me, Jessie. Fascinates me, intrigues me, gets me heated up to the ecstatic point, but what you said especially does not surprise me. You're a highly desirable woman, Jessica Starbuck."

and biting treatment. Soon he worked a line of kisses down her flat belly to the reddish triangle of her protective bush, where her shapely legs met.

She pulled him up and kissed his lips. "I'm halfway convinced to stay all night."

He kept her on top and pushed her legs apart, then lifted her and lowered her gently as she guided his pine-tree shaft upward to her waiting scabbard. She slid down all the way, and this time she provided the motive force.

Jessie rocked back and forth on his staff, and soon her knees found the bed and she powered forward and then reversed, riding him like a young pony.

The second time was more powerful, more rewarding. When the climaxes had ripped them apart and discarded them on the bed, they lay there panting, grinning.

"It couldn't be that good again," Jessie said.

"It was better than good. Now, before you get any sexy ideas again, I suggest we renew our energy with some cherry pie I bought today and some coffee. Any takers?"

They had pie and coffee in the bedroom, and Jessie laughed softly. "I don't know when I've felt more relaxed, as happy as a spring colt on the open range. I think staying here all night is the best idea that you've had all day."

Vince kissed her forehead. "It's a great idea, but how am I going to sneak you out of here in the morning without all my neighbors seeing you?"

"Easy. I don't plan on doing much sleeping the rest of the night. Then I'll be out of here before daylight, while your nosy neighbors are still snoring." Jessie reached over and kissed his inviting lips.

"Now, will you stop talking and treat a lady how a lady likes to be treated?"

Vince put the cups and saucers on the floor, well away from the bed, and they both fell backward onto the soft mattress. The night was far from over, and Jessie was determined to make good use of every second of it.

★

Chapter 11

The next morning, Ki knocked on Jessie's door as usual at seven for their breakfast. She answered at once, and they went to the Gold Mine Cafe.

Jessie smiled at Ki. "You look anxious to tell me something. What did you find out about Clatter?"

"I trailed him most of the afternoon and evening. He spent the night at the widow Agatha Blaine's house, and it wasn't a social call. I figure that gives Clatter a strong motive to kill off the husband, so he can have the widow."

"Clatter and the widow Blaine. That's interesting. I was at her house the other morning just after she'd had a hard night in bed. Clatter must have been there. Would Clatter kill Lawson at the Ready Relief mine?"

"Why not? It would throw suspicion on Maxwell and not involve Clatter."

Jessie nodded and worked on her breakfast. After a while she pointed her fork at Ki.

"I learned something else yesterday about Clatter. Vince told me that both Clatter and Maxwell have silent partners. Not generally known, but there are investors involved. Now, that means regular reports to the investors and sharing profits. Vince said in cases like these the operating partner has been known to skim money off the top like rich cream, before he figures the profit and loss statement. A man can get rich that way on a good mine, and the partners never know.

"If Lawson found out about the skimming, most likely at Maxwell's mine, it would be big trouble for Maxwell. He'd have to buy off Lawson to keep him quiet—or kill him. So we have another good motive for killing Lawson."

"It's also another one that's hard if not impossible to prove," Ki said. "We can't get in to look at the books. Anyway, any skimming would not show up on the books. It would take place in the smeltering shed before the gold bars were cast and stamped."

"Yes, and Lawson would have had a good chance to find out about it, working in the smeltering operation for that long."

They finished breakfast and went outside, into the high mountain sunshine. There was a nip in the October air, signaling the coming cold days. Julian sat a little over four thousand feet up the edge of the mountains.

"Let's check the telegraph office," Jessie said. "Something might be in for us from Wyoming."

At the small telegraph office, the key operator sorted through half a dozen envelopes and picked out one for Jessie.

She ripped it open and read the note inside, handwritten on a yellow sheet. Most of the telegraph offices had the new typewriters but not this one in Julian. The message read:

JESSIE STARBUCK, GEN. DELIVERY, JULIAN, CALIFORNIA. YES, REMEMBER LAWSON. WORKED WITH HIM HERE. HE ASKED ABOUT A WANTED FOR TRAVIS YOUNG. SENDING IT TO YOU BY MAIL. WANTED HERE FOR BANK ROBBERY AND MURDER. DESCRIPTION: SIX FEET TALL, 190 POUNDS, BROWN HAIR, BROWN MUSTACHE, GREEN EYES, BULLET SCAR ON LEFT ARM, TATTOO "ROSE" ON RIGHT SHOULDER. REWARD $2,000. MAIL WILL TAKE ABOUT A WEEK. KEEP ME INFORMED. DEPUTY SHERIFF CHICK ESKRIDGE.

Ki read the wire when Jessie handed it to him. "That description fits fifty men in town, except for the scar and tattoo."

Jessie grinned. "You hold down those fifty men and I'll rip off their shirts checking for the tattoo." She shook her head. "This isn't going to be a big help. I was hoping. We can check with the postmistress, but for sure this Travis Young changed his name when he came to town. Maybe he used his bank robbery money to buy into a mine or start a store here."

"All we've got is a bunch of maybes," Ki said. "Where are we going to find some solid evidence?"

"I wish I knew. Oh, Vince said the midget, Mr. Tall, who runs the Tall Saloon, was a good friend of Lawson's. Might be easier if you go over there and have a talk with him. Bartenders and saloon owners often know things the rest of the town doesn't."

Ki grinned. "I didn't think you minded barging into those mostly men-only saloons."

"I don't, but in this case, when we want to find out vital information, it's a time to be more subtle. You're good at that. I'd just raise a lot of eyebrows and find mostly silence."

Ki nodded and headed for the Tall Saloon. It was one of those in town that opened for the small morning trade. Only three men stood at the bar when Ki entered. Four more older men played cards at a back table. He didn't see any dance hall girls. They had probably worked late as usual and were sleeping in.

Behind the bar stood the small man. Ki ordered a draft beer and sipped it. He watched the midget moving up and down the bar on his special platform.

"Mr. Tall," Ki said. "I have a problem that I think you can help me with." Two of the men at the bar moved away from Ki. The midget came down the bar with small steps, curiosity on his face.

"A problem?"

"Yes. Where can we talk in private?"

"My quarters in back," Tall said. "Let me call my apron."

A few minutes later, Ki sat in a normal-size chair in the room in back of the bar. The room itself had been converted to the midget's size: a cut-down cookstove, a low table, small

98

chairs, and a bed with the legs cut off so the sagging springs almost touched the floor.

Mr. Tall sipped at a glass of apple cider from a local apple grower and looked up.

"You said your name was Ki. That's Japanese?"

"Yes, I'm half-Japanese and half-American."

"You mentioned a problem I could help you with."

Ki told him about coming to town to investigate the Lawson Blaine death.

"I understand you were a good friend of Lawson's."

The midget sipped the cider again and looked away. "Yes, he was a good man. Treated me as an equal, and few men do that. You must understand that feeling. You've probably been called a Japo before or a Chinaman. You understand. Lawson was a fine man, yes, and a good friend."

"We think he was murdered."

Grandy Tall looked up sharply. "Hadn't heard that before. Did seem a little strange, an inside worker killed by an ore car on the surface." The midget stared up at Ki. "You know this for sure?"

"Not yet. Hard evidence is difficult to find. Lawson's widow said he was about to take in a wanted man and make a two-thousand-dollar reward. Did he mention anything about that to you?"

"No. He came around once a week, usually on Saturday, and we'd have a beer and talk. Nothing important. He did mention he expected to be getting some big money. He didn't say how."

"Then he didn't talk about who the man was he was interested in capturing and sending back to Wyoming?"

"Not a word."

"Damn."

"You think this wanted man killed Lawson?"

"Best lead we have so far." Ki sipped at the beer. He liked this little man. He was honest, friendly. "Grandy, how did you come to be in Julian?"

Grandy finished his cider and laughed. "Why not Julian? Nice little town. The key word here is little. I grew up in San Francisco, and I've seen enough of big towns to last me for the rest of my life. Don't like them. Never did.

99

"Here there are fewer people to stare at me. By now most of the natives just treat me like anybody else. Newcomers are worse, but they settle in."

"You talk like an educated man."

"Had some book learning, too much probably. I found out that my mother worked. She was busy at night. I was nine when I figured out that she was Little Lulu, the tiniest whore in San Francisco. She was famous. I ran away from home and damned near starved. Three months later, I went back home.

"My dad was regular sized like you. He stayed with my mother through her best years. Then when I was ten, she was murdered and my father jumped off a building and killed himself."

"That must have been a shock," Ki said.

"It tore me apart. Later I learned that my dad had an inherited disease. The males in our family never lived to be more than thirty-five years old. He was over thirty-nine when he cheated the damn disease."

The midget snorted. "Yeah, I see you looking at me wondering. I'm thirty-two. I've decided to live life just as large and full as I can for whatever time I have left. Been here in town for over ten years now. Seen the boom times, this slower period. But things will pick up. Lots of gold out there yet."

"I hope there is," Ki said. "Living life to its fullest is a fine idea. Do it today. I like that. It has a Japanese flavor to it."

Grandy stared at Ki for a moment. "Are you a samurai?"

Ki smiled. "How did you know?"

"I've read a lot about the Japanese. Miss Starbuck did not appear to be your lover, and you go everywhere with her, so you must be her protector, her samurai, and she your master."

"You're probably the only one in town who knows that. You're a highly perceptive man."

"Not true, but I wish it were. Wish I had your discipline, your dedication, your centering. I haven't seen you fight, but I heard about the throwing stars. I envy you the skills you have mastered."

Ki bowed gracefully to the small man. "You honor me."

"Just wish Lawson had told me the man's name. Now that

100

I think on it, he said he was tracking down a bank robber. But he didn't tell me the name."

"Did Lawson have any other close friends he might have told the name to?"

"Guy Lawson worked with, name of Frenken, Earl Frenken. He might know."

Ki stood and thanked the small man. He bowed again, then reached out and shook Grandy's hand.

"Miss Starbuck appreciates your help. You keep right on living life as large as you can."

Someone coughed behind Ki. He turned around without appearing to rush but faced the other person in a split second. She was about his height, blond, almost pretty and with a generous body. She wore a soft blue dress that cost more than a saloon girl could afford.

"Ah, Jacqueline," Grandy Tall said. "I hoped you'd get back before Ki left. Jacqueline, this is my new Japanese friend Ki. He's an important and highly talented man."

They said hello and Grandy smiled. "This lovely lady helps me to stay sane and at the same time to live life large." He smiled. Ki nodded and left the room.

He continued out of the saloon and stood in the morning sun wishing he had the answer to the puzzle. How did the various pieces they had fit together? Or did they have enough pieces yet to make sense even with them all in place?

He saw Jessie on the far side of the street, coming out of the hardware store, and he hurried across to the other boardwalk.

Later that afternoon, just before six o'clock, Jessie and Ki walked up to the Frenkens' house and Ki knocked on the door. It was dark out by then, and Earl Frenken opened the door slowly, peering out.

"Who's there? What do you want?" Frenken held a lamp up so he could see outside.

"Mr. Frenken, I'm Jessie Starbuck, a good friend of Lawson Blaine. I and my friend, Ki, want to talk to you about him. We spoke to your wife about it before."

"Oh, yeah. She told me." Frenken moved back and opened

101

the door. Jessie and Ki entered the house, and Frenken nodded, his face grim.

Earl Frenken was of less than average height and slender. He wore freshly washed miner's denim pants and a matching shirt. He had washed himself clean of mine dust, and his hair was still damp. Frenken wore a full beard of rich black that he kept trimmed to half an inch all over his face and neck. Dark eyes evaluated the pair in front of him.

"Sit, sit down, pardon my manners. Not much used to company here."

They all sat, and Jessie looked up when she heard a baby cry.

"You want to talk about Lawson. I can't say much. I wasn't there. Lawson worked late that night, and they found him in the morning. Nothing could be done. He'd been dead for hours. Don't know how he got himself caught between two runaway ore cars."

"I don't think he did, Mr. Frenken," Jessie said. "I'm sure that someone killed him. What do you think?"

"Got myself a job, good job. Don't have to swing a hammer no more, and I like that. Don't ever say I talked to you. I'd get fired in a minute if he found out."

"If who found out, Mr. Frenken?"

"Maxwell, of course. He's tough and mean."

"How do you think Lawson died, Mr. Frenken?" Jessie asked.

Frenken took a long breath. "Ain't for me to say. He's gone. Best friend I had. Worked together two years."

"If he was murdered, don't you want to see the man who did it caught and punished?"

Frenken looked up, his face showing anger. "Yes, yes! But how can you prove it? At night, nobody around the smelter shed. Who's to say what happened?"

"Somebody knows," Ki said. "What about the gold robbery? Do you think Lawson's death is connected with the robbery in any way?"

"Don't understand. He was already dead two weeks when the robbery happened."

"Is there a chance Lawson found out about plans for the

102

robbery, maybe heard something he shouldn't, and since he knew about it, he was killed?"

"Could be," Frenken said.

"Did Maxwell come into the smeltering shed often?" Ki asked.

"He was almost always there when we worked. Watched every drop of gold like a vulture ready to pounce. He followed the amalgam out of the tunnel and into the pot, then watched the heating, pouring, and marking the bricks."

"Did Lawson stay after his regular shift often?" Jessie asked.

"Time and again. Maybe once a week. He would make sure that they had all of the gold bricks in place in the tunnel, check the guards with Mr. Maxwell, clean up, hunt for any spilled molten gold. He was all over the place."

"Did Maxwell talk about the gold shipment with you or Lawson?" Ki asked.

"No, never. He didn't know himself until the day that Wells Fargo decided to take a run. They picked up whatever gold was ready, made out the manifest, and it was gone. Everybody knows they collected the gold late at night. I was always gone. Worked there three years now and never did see a single one of them gold wagons come or go from the Ready Relief."

"Maybe Maxwell talked about the shipments when Lawson stayed late," Jessie suggested.

Frenken twisted in the chair. He stood and went to the lamp, turned up the wick until it smoked just a hint, then eased it down to a normal flame.

"Sure, he could have. The last few days before he died, Lawson seemed to be in good spirits. He was laughing, and even said he'd soon be able to buy a better horse for the five-mile ride out to the mine every day."

"Did he say why?"

"No. I asked him. Said it was his secret."

"Mr. Frenken, we've found out Lawson was working on capturing a man on a wanted poster with a two-thousand-dollar reward. Do you have any idea who he was going to take in?"

"A reward poster? Knew he'd been a lawman for a while. He didn't say nothing to me about any wanted. Two thousand dollars?"

"The name on the poster was Travis Young, but there's no one in town by that name. The wanted man must have changed his name, and we don't know who he is. He could be the man who killed Lawson."

Frenken shook his head. "The things you don't know about your good friends. Amazing. I'm afraid I've told you all I know about Lawson. Now, I'd appreciate it if you would leave. I don't want anybody dropping in and finding you here and reporting it to Maxwell. I hear he has spies all over town."

They thanked him and left. On the three-block walk to Main Street, they talked over their conversation with Frenken. They hadn't learned anything to help—with the exception that Lawson had been doing some night work after his shift.

"So there could be four motives," Jessie said. "Knowledge of the coming gold robbery, knowing about skimming profits off the top before reporting to the partners, the bank robber on the wanted poster and wanting Blaine's wife."

"Great, we have four motives and no suspects."

"We have at least two—Clatter and Maxwell."

"Now we have two suspects and no proof," Ki said. "That's just as bad."

They had a late supper at the Julian Cafe and pondered the problem.

"We've got to do something to surprise and worry the killer so he makes a stupid mistake," Jessie said.

"Like what?"

"I'm thinking." Jessie stared into her coffee cup and set it down quickly.

"We can call for a meeting of the mining committee. There's no practical law enforcement in the Julian mining district, so legally we can call for a mining committee meeting to present evidence in the murder of Lawson Blaine and name the killer, who will be brought to trial by the mining committee."

"Can we do that?"

"We can try," Jessie said. "Let's go see if Vince is still in his office. If there's a mining committee here, Vince will know. Even if there isn't one and it isn't legal, we can still put up notices all over town that we're going to do it and wait and see if anyone tries to stop it. That way we might be able to smoke out the killer."

★

Chapter 12

Vince Hirlbach looked up in surprise at the two visitors who stepped into his office. Five minutes later he stared at Jessie and Ki and shook his head.

"You can't be serious. A miner's committee court and a trial? This isn't 1850, during the gold rush up at Sutter's Mill you know. We have a legal county government, a sheriff and a district attorney. We even have a justice of the peace for minor offenses right here in Julian. Miner's courts were for areas where there wasn't even a territory yet so they had no kind of law enforcement."

Jessie smiled and touched his hand across the desk. "Vince, that's the beauty of it. I'll hit hard on the fact that the local law enforcement isn't working. No inquiry into the murder of Lawson, no investigation by the other legal bodies, so we'll go back to the miner's court and miner's justice. Of course it's ninety percent sham and bluff, but we might just make it sound real enough so the killer will make a wrong move or do something dumb like try to kill Ki and me. Then we'd have a good strong lead we could run down."

"If you aren't over at the undertaker's on a big slab of pine wood." Vince stood and paced his office. He frowned, held his hands clasped behind his back, and marched over to the window and then back.

"We have a mining district committee, that's all legal and proper. I'm not too sure just what it does, but we have one. Why don't you use that name and see what you can stir up?"

"Who is on the committee?" Jessie asked. "Will we be stepping on anybody's toes this way? Maybe we should talk to them first and tell them what we're doing so they won't immediately come out with a denial."

Vince rubbed his face with one hand. "Oh, boy, I was afraid you would ask me that. It's been a while since they've met. I know two of them are mine owners, two are working miners, and I think the other one is a merchant. Five as I recall. Let me go talk to some people, and I'll come back with the names."

"Meet you in the hotel lobby in an hour?" Jessie asked.

"That should be fine. Then perhaps we could go out for a dessert or coffee somewhere."

"Sounds good. I'll go write up what we want on the flyer. Does the *Julian Sentinel* do job printing as well?"

"James Jasper is the editor and publisher, and he does printing. That's probably what keeps him in business. He knew Lawson. I'm sure you'll have no problem with him about printing the flyers in the morning."

Jessie and Ki left and headed for the hotel. Ki spoke up at the hotel steps.

"Will you be needing me for a while? I have to go see somebody."

Jessie laughed softly. "It wouldn't by any chance be that cute little waitress, Happy, at the cafe, would it?"

Ki nodded. "I just remembered I forgot to leave her a tip." He turned and hurried away.

In the hotel Jessie went up to her room, found paper and a pencil, and worked on the flyer she would tack up around town in the morning.

She wrote it once, then marked out some words and did it again. When she was satisfied, she read it once more to be certain.

"PUBLIC NOTICE. The Julian Mining District Committee will meet at noon on October 12, to consider a petition for committee justice action against the man or men who murdered

106

Lawson Blaine some two weeks ago.

"Since neither the County of San Diego nor the Julian Village Marshal has taken any action on this dastardly crime, the Mining District Committee feels it must consider the charges, then if necessary arrest the suspect and hold a trial commencing immediately. The case will be resolved before midnight, October 12, and any sentence of the guilty will be carried out the following day.

"Anyone having information about the murder of Lawson Blaine is asked to be on hand for the public meeting of the Committee at noon in the Wilberforce Saloon and to take part in these much needed and entirely legal proceedings."

Jessie left it unsigned. She went down to the lobby and had to wait only fifteen minutes before Vince arrived.

"Let's go see this James Jasper and get him to do the printing for us tonight," Jessie said. "I'll pay him double his usual charges. I'm going to have some boys tack these notices up all over town by eight o'clock tomorrow morning."

On the way to the printer, they talked over what Vince had learned about the committee.

"The Julian Mining District Committee is a legal group but empowered only to set up standards for claims, to appoint a registrar, and to hear complaints about claim jumping and a few other claims procedures.

"I spotted Oliver Pierpoint. He's one of the miners on the committee. I asked him who the other men were, and he told me. Then I explained what we're trying to do. He nearly fell on the boardwalk laughing. He said it would be a great joke on the committee. Most folks still think the committee has hanging powers, but it doesn't. He said full speed ahead. He thought there was something fishy about Blaine's death as well, but nothing could be proved."

"At least we can make a try at shaking up the killers," Jessie said. "I have some ideas how to make ourselves 'available' to anyone who wants to try to do us in."

Vince looked at her quickly.

"Don't worry, we'll be safe enough, but this should give the bad guys a chance to show their hand. That's when we take over."

107

James Jasper, editor, publisher, and printer, sat in his window office at the newspaper building working with pencil on paper. Vince knocked on the window and motioned that they wanted to come inside.

A few moments later Jasper looked up from the notice Jessie had given him to read.

"Can't be done," the editor said. "The Julian Mining District Committee doesn't have these powers." The editor was a compact man with a stiff white collar. He worked with his suit coat on and wore spectacles, his bushy hair parted in the middle and combed to both sides, giving his head a wider, bolder look than most men's.

Jessie nodded. "I'm quite aware of that, Mr. Jasper. But not everyone in town will be. Lots of men here remember the rough days of mining committee justice and will come to the meeting to see what happens.

"What I'm trying to do is flush out the man or men who killed Lawson Blaine. He was murdered and not killed in an accident. I suspect that you were not convinced with the story of his death out at the Ready Relief mine, but you did nothing about it. I want to post these notices all over town tonight or early tomorrow morning."

"What kind of results are you expecting, Miss Starbuck?" the editor asked.

"I fully expect someone will try to kill me."

The editor leaned back in his chair as if he had been struck. "You expect someone to try to kill you?"

"Yes. I won't let them, and I and my friend, Ki, will capture the man or men and find out who hired them and work our way back to the man who killed Lawson Blaine."

The editor rocked in his chair a moment. Then he laid down his pencil, picked up a green eyeshade, and put it on.

"We better get started setting type if I'm to get this printed for you before midnight. How many copies do you want?"

For the next two hours Jessie watched the printer and publisher at work. He set the type from letters he took from assigned spots in a case and stood on a "stick." Soon the letters made words and spaces and then whole sentences.

He bound the letters and spaces and spacers between the

lines together tightly, tapped then down even and flat with a rubber block and a hammer, and then pulled a proof.

Jessie read it quickly and found one error, and Jasper corrected it. Then he printed the flyer on his small "job" press. It was one of the newer types and more automatic than some. It had a roller that inked the type between each printing, but it still had to be cranked over each time by hand.

He printed fifty copies on heavy yellow paper and provided Jessie with a box of quarter-inch tacks and two hammers.

"No sense waiting until morning," she said. "Vince, let's get to tacking up some notices."

They covered the downtown area, putting a notice on the outside of every business, near the entrance and on the wall facing the boardwalk. They put them on the bulletin boards some of the stores had set up and then tacked the rest on fences and trees.

Jessie kept two of them. She'd put one in Ki's key box at the hotel.

Vince laughed about what the other four Julian Mining District Committee members would say when they saw the notice. "I figure they'll wonder if they still have the power, and will get together in a rush to decide. The whole town will be buzzing with this shortly after breakfast."

"Which reminds me that I better get back to the hotel for some rest," Jessie said. "Tomorrow could be an interesting and an exciting day."

"Want some coffee and pie at my place?" Vince asked.

Jessie squeezed his arm but shook her head. "Last night was marvelous, but now I have to get ready for business. I need to be prepared for anything tomorrow, or maybe even tonight. You can help me push the dresser over in front of my hotel room window. I don't want some killer to throw a stick of dynamite into my room at dawn."

At the hotel they went up the stairs separately. Jessie was first and had her door open when Vince arrived. He tugged the dresser in front of the window and made sure there was a chair that would fit under the door handle.

109

"You sure you don't want me to stay?" he asked. "I can sleep on the floor."

Jessie shook her head, sending her coppery blond hair flying. "Not tonight, Vince. Ki will be back soon, and the two of us can take care of anything these yahoos can throw at us. I doubt if it will be tonight. It might take some time for the killer to hear about the notices."

She kissed Vince good night at the door and edged him into the hall. He waved and hurried away.

Ki knocked on her door a half hour later. He showed her the notice. "You had any visitors yet?" he asked.

"No. I really don't expect any tonight. It'll take time for people to see the notices, read them, and then get back to the men who did the killing. Probably no reaction until morning. Then both of us have to be 'available' for the bad guys at least to shoot at."

"A dummy in a chair by the window?" Ki asked.

"That's one. A stroll down the boardwalk with frequent stops behind other people and wagons, and in stores."

"I'll sleep here tonight, on the floor, just in case of some excitement," Ki said.

Jessie knew there was no arguing with him. She saw Ki turn his back. She slipped out of her clothes and into bed. She tossed Ki a pillow and one blanket from the bed. He settled down on the floor and in a minute went to sleep. Jessie knew the slightest noise at the door or the window and Ki would be awake and ready to repel any attack.

When Jessie awoke at six A.M., Ki was gone. She dressed in her riding clothes, strapped on her gunbelt and her .38 revolver, and was ready to go to breakfast when Ki knocked on the door.

"Let's rig up a dummy with your shirt and hat," he said. "We can stuff your shirt with a sheet from the bed."

In ten minutes they had a fair-looking replica made of Jessie. Ki pulled the dresser away from the window, and they put the dummy in the chair, with the hat and shoulders showing over the top. They pushed the chair over beside the window and then parted the thin curtains. From the street, they thought, it should look natural enough.

110

"We can leave it only for an hour or so at a time," Jessie said.

They hurried downstairs and out the side door, breakfast forgotten. Ki pointed them to hiding places in the alley directly across from the hotel. They checked the second-floor windows and saw Jessie's dark brown, flat-topped hat and a pair of shoulders extending over the top of the chair. They nodded and started their watch of the street and alley.

Nothing had happened by eight o'clock that morning. They had seen a lot of men stop and read the yellow notices. One man tore the flyer off a building and marched up the street.

"Must be one of the men on the mining committee," Jessie said. The man went into a store and didn't come out.

As the sun crawled higher, little knots of men gathered around some of the yellow notices talking and waving their arms.

"Looks like you have their attention," Ki said. "I'm going for a walk up that way. Since you're still sitting in your window, you can't be on the street yet." He grinned. "Just don't get in any trouble down here."

Ki came out of the alley and hurried up the street toward a group of men. He stood at the back of ten or twelve who were talking.

"The committee can't do that anymore," one man said. "Mining committee law was when we didn't have no law here."

"We don't have no law here," another man shouted. "When you seen the sheriff or even a deputy up here in Julian?"

"So Blaine was murdered," another man said. "Never believed that story about him being crushed by an ore car. Damn convenient. Why would somebody want to kill Blaine?"

Ki drifted off to the next bunch of men and a few women gathered outside the general store.

"Like old times," a miner said. "We really called the shots back then. Had more law than Julian has right now, I'd say. I'm going to support the mining committee."

Ki worked back toward the alley across from the hotel. He listened to more talk, and most of it was favorable. One

111

man claimed to be on the committee and said he didn't know anything about any such idea.

Ki was still half a block away from where Jessie waited when he heard two rifle shots. At the same moment glass shattered and he saw Jessie's hotel window vanish inward. He took off on a sprint down the street, checking for any white smoke from the rifle rounds.

He saw what he figured was a trace of smoke near the alley where he had left Jessie.

By the time he raced into the alley, he knew he was too late. Jessie was gone. In the dust, he read the tracks. Somebody had surprised her from behind. He found the two rifle casings. The tracks led through the alley. Ki turned and ran, following the prints. Jessie's boot tracks didn't show at all. Somebody was carrying her.

He made it halfway down the alley with stores backing up on each side but leaving a twenty-to forty-foot-wide stretch in the middle. A rifle snarled from the alley's far end. Ki dove to the left and came up behind the stub end of a building and out of the line of fire. Two more rounds chipped wood off the corner of the wall that protected him.

Ki looked around the foundation at ankle level. The rifleman was gone from the street. Ki sprinted down to the end of the alley and looked both ways. He didn't see Jessie anywhere. Then he spotted a closed carriage moving at a walk away from him. A long line of freight wagons had been parked along the near side of the street. Ki raced to the first heavy wagon and watched the carriage. It still moved at a slow walk.

He ran forward, dodging behind the freight wagons as he went. He had a twenty-foot space to cross with no protection. A rifle poked out the rear of the carriage and fired twice at him. He zigzagged, and both rounds missed. Then he was behind another string of freight wagons with their high box sides shielding him like a wall.

The carriage picked up speed. A man opened the side curtain and aimed a shotgun at Ki from no more than thirty feet. Ki's right hand powered forward, sending a *shuriken* throwing star spinning on its way.

112

The star dug into the gunman's wrist before he could fire. His reaction to the spurting blood from his wrist sent a load of buckshot into the ground beside the carriage, and the man screamed and vanished inside the rig.

Ki raced ahead until he was even with the carriage. A man sat on the high seat, driving a pair of blacks. Ki's second star sliced deeply into the driver's left shoulder. The man screamed, dropped the reins, and fell off the carriage. The team slowed and, with no direction from the slack reins, soon stopped.

Ki crouched behind another freight wagon. No sound came from the carriage.

Ki waited. After another minute of no response, someone in the rig pulled the side curtain open. Jessie showed, kneeling, with a dark shadow behind her. A man's arm was around her throat, and his right hand held a six-gun muzzle to the side of her head.

"Bastard foreign devil!" the man in the carriage bellowed. "You hurt us, but we have the upper hand. We have Jessie Starbuck, and you back off or she's dead in ten seconds. I want to see you drop those damn stars and run back the way you came. Do it now, or Jessie is just another pretty corpse and you're out of a job."

Ki stood behind the wagon so his shoulders and head showed over the top.

"You win. I'm going. Don't hurt her. She hasn't done anything to you. Let her go, and we'll be out of town on the first stage."

The man behind Jessie hesitated. Ki saw Jessie bring her right arm forward slowly; then with a scream of fury she drove her elbow backward into the man behind her. Her elbow powered into his belly just below the ribs and blasted half the wind out of him. A moment later Jessie dove out of the carriage, hit the dust of the street hard with both hands, bent her head, and landed on her right shoulder. She rolled three times in the street, came to her feet, and darted for the protection of the freight wagons.

One shot came from the dark interior of the carriage. Ki threw one star at the void, raced for the back of the rig, and caught it just as someone started the horses moving.

113

Jessie watched as Ki tore through the rear of the carriage with his *tanto* knife and flattened as two shots blasted through the same black canvas. Then Ki dove into the opening, and a few moments later the rig stopped.

Jessie waited. For almost a minute there was no movement from the black rig, then Ki caught the reins of the carriage, turned it around, and drove over to Jessie.

"Miss, would you like a ride? We're going into the countryside, where we can have some privacy for a long talk with our new friends in the backseat. He's promised to tell us all sorts of interesting things, if he can leave town directly after our little chat."

★

Chapter 13

Jessie stepped into the carriage and saw two men in back holding their wounds. They were the ones who had caught her by surprise in the alley. She pushed one aside and picked up her gunbelt and her .38 revolver. After checking the loads, she pushed the weapon into leather.

"Who hired you?" Jessie asked, stabbing her finger into the shoulder of the closest of the two.

"Nobody. We wanted a ransom for you. You're rich." The shorter of the two said the words, but they lacked conviction.

"He's the uncooperative one," Ki said. He drove the rig down the street, back to Main, and then took the south road out of town.

Five minutes later he pulled to the side of the trail, into a flat space, and drove a hundred yards behind some small trees and out of sight of the road.

"Out, both of you," Ki commanded. The men looked at him, then climbed out of the carriage, groaning in pain from their wounds. Blood smeared one man's right wrist and arm. He held the gash with his other hand. The taller man had blood on his chest and left arm where Ki's throwing stars had punctured him. Ki had not used killing throws. They needed these two alive.

When all four were on the ground behind the carriage, Ki

faced the two wounded men. "The lady asked who hired you. She expects an answer. If you don't cooperate, it will bring swift and painful results."

The smaller man with the bloody wrist screeched in pain. "You said you'd take us to the doctor."

"After you cooperate," Jessie said. "I want to know who hired you." There was a fierce anger in her words, and both men looked at her at once. The larger man shrugged.

"Don't know him. Gave us fifty dollars in the saloon and furnished us with the rifle and the carriage. Said to kill you both and we'd get another hundred and fifty."

"What was the man's name?" Ki demanded.

"He didn't say. I didn't ask. It was business."

"Business?" Jessie asked.

The tall man shrugged again. "Nothing personal. We didn't know either of you. Just a way to make some money."

Ki snorted. He looked at Jessie. "Will you give me fifty dollars to kill this larger man?"

Jessie nodded. "Yes, go ahead. He isn't any use to us. After all, it's just business."

Ki took out his *tanto*, the short curve-bladed knife, from the lacquered sheaf thrust in the waistband of his denim pants. He tested the edge for a moment, then took two quick steps toward the larger man and made a quick slicing thrust an inch from the man's throat.

"It could be all over for you right now," Jessie said. "You realize you could be bleeding to death from a slit throat even before you fell to the ground?"

The man jolted backward just after the warning with the *tanto*. His eyes went wide, and he caught his throat with his right hand.

"No! No. I told you I'd cooperate."

"Describe the man who hired you," Ki spat.

"He was short, small, maybe five four. Wore a town suit and a string tie. No hat. Black hair. Had spectacles. Talked like a city man, big words."

"When were you to meet him?" Jessie asked.

"Right after we done it. Before noon at the same place, the Tall Saloon."

"Go check on him," Jessie said. "I'll take these two to the marshal." Ki turned and ran toward town.

She gave Ki a five minute head start, then put the two men in the carriage and drove to the marshal's office and his small lockup.

Jessie marched the two bloody men into the jail with her .38 in her hand. Marshal Zane looked up in surprise from his checkerboard.

"What the hell?"

"I have two prisoners for you, Marshal. I'm filing a complaint against them for attempted murder, and murder for hire."

"You're that Starbuck woman, right?"

"Correct, Marshal. I suggest you hold these men and notify the county sheriff to pick them up for trial. If you don't do that, or if for any reason these men escape your custody, I'll be filing similar charges against you as an accomplice. Do I make myself perfectly clear on this matter?"

The checkerboard became unimportant to Marshal Zane. He stood and motioned to the two prisoners.

"Into the back room. I'll get you locked up and then send for the doc. Looks like you got cut up some." A minute later the marshal came back to the main room.

"Miss Starbuck, I've got them in the cell. Nasty wounds. Doc Raleigh will be over directly. Now, you want to do some paperwork with me? Sheriff always demands paperwork on any prisoner. We'll need the exact circumstances of the crime. You know those men's names?"

A block up the street Ki eased into the rear door of the Tall Saloon and checked over the patrons. He found two small men, one at the bar and one playing cards by himself at a table. Only the man at the table wore a suit and string tie.

Before the man could look up, Ki straddled a chair opposite him and put his *tanto* on the man's hand that held the cards.

"I need to talk with you in the alley. If you would be so kind as to come with me."

The small man's eyes went cold. He eased back in his chair.

"Ain't about to go nowhere, not with the likes of you."

117

The curved blade turned and sliced a quarter of an inch across the back of the man's hand. Ki rose and moved beside the man, the blade touching his throat.

"I'd be much obliged if you'd come along. Be a shame to get your blood all over Mr. Tall's saloon. You won't be in any shape to wipe it up for him."

Ki moved the blade to the man's chin and lifted. The small man stood slowly as the pressure by the blade under his chin increased. He walked ahead of Ki toward the back door.

"Somebody help me!" the man wailed.

One of the drinkers at the bar reached for his six-gun. Grandy Tall leveled a sawed-off shotgun at him across the bar.

"Best let those two have their discussion out back, friend," Grandy said softly. "Now, put your hands on the bar and finish your drink, or I'll blow your worthless carcass into two pieces."

Ki herded the small man out the back door, then patted his jacket and legs but found no hideout weapon. He spun him around and pushed him against the building.

"They missed."

"What are you talking about?"

Ki swung a backhanded slap that gently grazed the man's cheek. "Let's not waste time. Your two men missed. I know it and now you know it. What I want to find out is who hired you."

"Don't . . . don't hit me. I can't stand that. It was supposed to be easy."

Ki held the *tanto* in front of the man's face, then balanced it on one finger. "Who hired you?"

"I can't tell you that. He'd kill me himself. Ask me anything else."

Ki eased the blade against the man's cheek, then moved it slowly toward his left eye.

"Have you ever thought about how it would be to live the rest of your misspent life as a blind man?"

The blade edged closer and closer to his eye.

"Nooooooooooooooooooooo!" The one word came out a long wail. The small man swallowed, his eyes wide in shock and fear. "All right, I'll tell you."

118

A rifle barked down the alley. Before the gunman had a chance to chamber a second round, Ki dove to his left, behind the outhouse and a large stack of wooden boxes. When he looked back at the small man, he had been slammed back against the saloon wall. He still stood. Both his hands held his chest where a river of blood poured through his fingers. Another rifle shot blasted from partway down the alley, and the small man at the wall screamed as the round hit his chest. Then the sound died, and he slumped to the side, and a death-rattle last breath gushed from his lungs.

Ki had protection from the rifleman. Three more shots jolted into the outhouse and the heavy wooden boxes; then all went quiet.

Ki waited another three minutes. He was checkmated. There was no way he could go after the bushwhacker. His source was dead. It was the end of this line of attack. By now the killer would be two blocks away. Ki ran to the back door of the saloon and slipped inside. He told the midget what had happened.

Grandy Tall nodded. "I'll send word to the marshal, but likely he won't do anything. Nobody can blame you for that man's death; you never carry a gun."

Ki left the saloon by the front door and hurried down to the marshal's office. The black carriage sat on the street outside the law office, with blood on the seats.

Inside Ki found Jessie finishing the paperwork.

"See that this all gets to the sheriff on the next stage," she ordered. "He's got to come up here and attend to business."

Outside, on the boardwalk, Ki looked at the sun.

"Nearly noon. We going to the big miner's committee meeting?"

"After what you told me about the man who died in the alley, I wonder if there's any point in it now. We had our chance, and somebody made a countermove. Now there's no way we can trace who hired the man who paid the two bushwhackers. The bad guys are still one move ahead of us."

They walked half a block up Main and saw a small crowd outside the Wilberforce Saloon. Jessie grinned. "Let's see what's happening. If the saloon is overflowing, there must be a few people interested in the meeting."

They walked to the edge of the crowd, and soon a man came pushing his way out of the saloon. He eyed the people for a moment, then went to the street and jumped up on a wagon box and called to them.

"Over here. More of you out here than inside. You know me. I'm Oliver Pierpoint. I'm one of five men on the Julian Mining District Committee. Now, I want to tell you about those yellow notices.

"Actually the mining committee had nothing to do with them. Some folks still think it's a good idea. Maybe we can stir up the sheriff and get him up here. Every other town the size of ours has a deputy sheriff stationed there permanently, but not Julian.

"Now, for the Lawson Blaine death. A lot of folks think the man was murdered. We have some motives and some suspects, but nothing final yet. Just bear with us. We ain't gonna have no trial today. Not a chance. But if any of you know anything about the Blaine death, you come over here and tell me, or put it in writing and give it to me.

"If the man was murdered, then by damn I want to see that justice is done and his killer is found and convicted. Outside of that, we're still a mining committee, not a lawman committee. Let's see what you have to say."

Pierpoint dropped down off the wagon and talked to the people around him. One or two pushed forward to get to the committee man, but there wasn't a rush.

Vince ambled up beside Jessie and Ki. "At least the town got stirred up about something. Nobody's been so excited in this place since the last mine started producing rich ore."

"Will it do any good?" Jessie asked.

"Have to wait and see," Vince said. "You hear that a Wells Fargo investigator is in town?"

"Checking out the gold robbery?" Ki asked.

"True. He told me he wants to talk to both of you. You found the tracks and the two bodies. He got that from the sheriff, so evidently Marshal Zane sent a report to San Diego on the stage."

"What we found out there won't help catch the robbers and killers, but we'll be glad to talk to the man," Ki said.

120

"Good. He told me if I found you to see him at the Wells Fargo office as soon as you could."

Ki looked at Jessie.

"We better get over there," she said. "Looks like the big noontime meeting has played itself out."

The crowd around the saloon broke up as Ki and Jessie walked through it toward the Wells Fargo office, across from the hotel, where the stage came in and left every day. Inside, the office wasn't much more than a ticket counter and a place for what little freight got shipped by the stage line. Sending freight on the stage was expensive, and most goods came in on the slow wagons out of San Diego.

A man behind the ticket window looked up. "Yes, folks, what can I do for you?"

Someone else came from behind the speaker and stared at Ki.

"You must be the man who found the two dead stage robbers. That was some fine work. I'm Irving Davis. Usually I work out of San Francisco, but I was in San Diego when this robbery happened."

"Mr. Davis, this is my employer, Jessie Starbuck. Yes, my name is Ki, and we found the trail and the tracks and the bodies. I told the marshal, who evidently told the county sheriff."

"Anything else you've figured out since then?" Davis asked. "You seem to be quite a detective yourself."

Jessie shook her head. "Mr. Davis, we haven't come up with much that could help you. We have decided that since the gold runs are arranged the same afternoon they are made, the robbers would have to have been people who could be certain of the timing. That could be some employees of any of the mines shipping gold, a manager, even a mine owner."

Davis looked at her in surprise. "Well now, we had considered some of the employees of the mines, but I hadn't even thought it might be one of the mine owners. Stealing from themselves wouldn't really be that, would it, not with the guarantee. Interesting."

He watched them a moment, then waved them into the back room, which was an office with a door. They went inside, and Davis closed the door.

"Actually we don't want it to get around, but there was more gold on that shipment than I first thought. The manifest showed a total of almost sixty thousand dollars' worth."

"A worker in the tunnels makes two dollars a day, or about six hundred dollars a year," Ki said. "That shipment would be as much as a miner could earn in a hundred years."

"Now, there's an incentive," Davis said. "But who did it, who organized it, and who killed those two men who helped him? The marshal said the two dead men were identified as a pair of saloon swampers who hadn't been in town more than a week."

"Cheap help," Jessie said.

"Tomorrow I'll be going out and checking the gold bricks in each of the mines. They let us in to do that. Each brick has the date of casting and the special mark of the mine that smelts it. Which means these particular gold bricks can be identified if anyone tries to sell them whole."

"So the robber has to melt down the gold and sell it a little at a time," Ki said.

"Or melt it down and put a new date and a new mine stamp into it," the Wells Fargo man said. "That's what interested me when you mentioned that it could be an owner. All he would need to do is melt down the bricks and restamp them with his mine's mark and put on a new date."

"How many mines shipped gold that night?" Jessie asked.

"Eight of them, all the biggest and most productive. They're the ones who produce more, so they ship more. At least I don't have to check on twenty-four separate mine operations. I start in the morning on the eight shippers."

Jessie smiled at the detective. "Mr. Davis, we'll work with you on whatever we can. We're here on another matter, but if there is any tie-in to the gold robbery, you'll know everything we do."

"Thanks. I better let you get on with your own case. A murder investigation, I hear."

"Right," Ki said. They shook hands with Davis, said they would keep in touch, and went out to the street. They walked directly to the hotel and had lunch, then went upstairs to Jessie's room.

122

She paced the small area, hands behind her back. "We have a new problem. Whoever hired the man who hired the two bushwhackers is still out there and can try again at any time. We better switch rooms for tonight without letting the room clerk or anyone else know it."

Ki nodded. "We'll find vacant rooms and move in for the night. No sense in sitting here waiting for them to come."

"Will someone come, Ki?"

"If I were in the killer's shoes, I'd try again. Both of us are a danger to whoever killed Blaine. Now the whole town is in on the murder, and the killer must be furious. I'd say we take it easy, stay off the streets as much as we can, and not move around too much at night."

"What can we prove that way, Ki?"

"We can stay alive and outthink the killer."

"Maybe that wanted poster will come from Wyoming."

Ki snapped his fingers. "We could ask Widow Blaine to search through the house. There just might be the copy of the poster there that the deputy sent to Lawson."

Jessie nodded. "We should get out there this afternoon. By the back way."

A half hour later they had left the hotel by the side entrance, worked down the alley and over two streets, and then gone two blocks uphill, farther than they had to, and come to Lawson Blaine's house from the rear.

Jessie went to the back porch and knocked on the door. Ki followed her, and Agatha Blaine opened the door a moment later.

"Oh, good. I was wondering about what you had found out."

Jessie and Ki went into the kitchen, sat at the table away from the windows, and told her as much as they had figured so far. It wasn't a lot.

"Agatha, would you have any idea if Lawson received a copy of a wanted poster from Wyoming? The deputy sheriff there said he sent one to Lawson at his request."

"A wanted poster? What does it look like?"

"Most of them are about eighteen inches high and maybe a foot wide and printed on some heavy paper stock, almost like cardboard."

123

"Land sakes, I ain't seen nothing like that," Agatha said.

"Could we help you take another look?" Jessie asked. "It could be with some of Lawson's things."

"He did have a table where he did his dreaming, he called it. He wanted to start a mine of his own, but he said first he'd have to find a strike, then get the money. That Lawson was a dreamer."

They spent a half hour going through the stacks on Lawson's table and two boxes of papers, but didn't find a poster.

At the back door, Jessie touched the widow's shoulder. "You keep looking, Agatha. It's terribly important. It could be the clue to who killed Lawson."

"I'll keep at it. Guess it could be anywhere."

"That's the problem," Jessie said.

They took a roundabout route back to the hotel.

"Looks like a wasted afternoon," Ki said. "I feel like a long run in this mountain air."

Jessie waved him off. "See you for supper, maybe."

It was just after dark when Irving Davis left the Wells Fargo office. He had all of his plans laid out. He knew the mines he would visit the next day, had a list of questions for each of the owners, and managers, or whoever loaded the bricks in the gold wagon.

Next on his schedule was a good supper at the best eatery in town. He considered the small selection, picked one, and ate. When he came out of the cafe a little after seven, he was intent only on getting a good night's sleep, to be ready for his big day tomorrow.

Davis paced along the boardwalk at an even stride. He was a man of action, and this case was looking more and more complicated all the time. He had asked to be assigned to it with three wires to San Francisco. At last the go-ahead had come through, and here he was.

The pair who'd found the bodies were a curious lot. He couldn't make them out. The Japanese said that the pretty lady was his employer. He had heard the name Starbuck for years, having been born and raised in San Francisco. He wondered if she were any relation to

124

one of San Francisco's most famous businessmen, Alex Starbuck.

He shook his head. Probably not. This pretty lady came from Texas. If he had had this case wrapped up, he wouldn't have minded spending a day trying to get to know that great lady a little better.

Irving Davis chuckled and stepped down to the dirt of an alley.

"Hey, you," somebody growled at him from the edge of the alley.

Davis turned, but saw no one in the darkness.

"Yeah, you, wife stealer! You low-down cheating bastard!"

Davis whirled toward the sound. "What are you talking about? Come out where I can see you."

His only answer was four revolver shots. Three of the rounds struck him in the chest, and he went down, thrown backward six feet by the impact of the big slugs hitting him at nearly the same time. Irving Davis died before anyone could reach his side.

★

Chapter 14

Ki finished a long series of exercises and body moves in his hotel room, to strengthen himself and keep his muscles flexible. He sat on the edge of the bed and breathed hard for a minute, then stood and began another series of workouts in the *te* martial arts.

Four quick raps sounded on his door. Ki frowned for a moment, then crossed the room. It wasn't Jessie's knock. He opened the door a crack so he could see who it was, then swung the door wide.

Sally Wondersome stood there, tears rolling down her cheeks, eyes red, long hair messed, and clothes awry.

"Please let me come in," she pleaded softly. "I'm in big trouble and I don't know what to do."

Ki leaned forward in a short bow, caught her hand, and helped her inside. He closed the door, and Sally put her arms around him and fell against his chest.

"I don't know where to go, who I can trust. Both of them hate me. What can I do, Ki? How can I get out of this mess?"

Gently he took her arms from him and led her to the bed. He sat her down, then pulled up the one wooden chair and sat in front of her.

"Sally, I can't help when I don't know what you're talking about. Please explain what you mean."

She dried her eyes. "Pull the shade on the window, please," she said softly. "I can't take a chance someone might see me here."

"No one will hurt you, Sally. Now, tell me why you're so frightened."

"Clatter, J. D. Clatter. I . . . I do some work for him now and then." She lifted her brows. "All right, I'm a lookout for him, a spy. I watch certain people and tell him what they do. It worked out well, but then somebody else wanted me to spy for him.

"More money, why not, I figured. Only he wanted me to spy on Clatter and tell him everything the man did. I decided to. I was working for Clatter and for Washington Maxwell at the same time. Somehow they found out. One of them or both of them, I don't know. Both of them are vicious, unscrupulous."

She leaned forward and kissed Ki's lips. "Oh, yes, that's good. I haven't felt this safe for weeks. Nobody saw me come into the hotel or up here to your room." Her expression of hope faded. Fear and mistrust and anger replaced it. "Ki, what am I going to do? How can I go on living here?"

It was still early in the evening. Ki figured maybe eight o'clock.

"You better not go back to your place. You'll have to stay the night here. The stage leaves at seven in the morning. You better be on it. Don't go back to your loft for clothes or anything. Someone probably is watching it. Stay here and then get on the stage and ride down to San Diego. There's always a spot for a girl with your looks and talents in San Diego."

Sally sighed. "I know you're right. I just hate to run out of another town. Gets to be a habit. I know I have to leave. Hell, messed up my life again."

"You must know a lot about both Clatter and Maxwell."

"I do. They think I know too much. One of them sent two men to beat me up this afternoon. I saw them coming and ran down to the general store before they could catch me. I've been in there for hours talking to the owner, to anyone who came in. The toughs wouldn't come in and get me. I finally got away out the back door when one of them went for supper."

Ki nodded. "I have some questions for you to answer. First, do you know if either of the men had anything to do with Lawson Blaine's murder?"

Her eyes went wide. "Oh, no, that's not the kind of thing they talk about. Nothing about that."

"Do you think either man is skimming gold off the top of the pile before he reports to his partners?"

"Skimming off the cream. Sure, both of them are. Not enough to get caught at, but they have plenty of gold put away where they can get it."

"What about the Wells Fargo gold wagon robbery? Do you know if either man had anything to do with it?"

Her eyes opened wide again, and she gaped at Ki. "The gold wagon robbery. Oh. I figured that was some outlaws. Neither of them has even talked about it. I guess the gold is all protected by Wells Fargo so they'll have to pay off. . . ."

"But neither of them mentioned anything about it before or after it happened?"

"Not a word, not to me. Not when we were in bed. Most men talk a lot when they make love. Nothing about the robbery."

"Curious." Ki moved the chair and sat beside her on the bed. "You feeling better?"

"Ever so much. But I know you're right about leaving town. Why would one of them want to hurt me?"

"You must know something they don't want you to. One of them might have slipped in talking about it. Might be about the robbery, or a murder."

"Wish I knew what it was. Oh, did you hear about the murder on the street tonight? The Wells Fargo detective here from San Francisco to investigate the gold robbery was shot down on Main Street. Right near an alley. Somebody said he had three bullets in the chest."

"The gold wagon robber is getting nervous," Ki said in distress. "Why else would he kill the detective from Wells Fargo?"

Sally reached for him, hugged him tightly. "Hold me, Ki. Make me feel safe. I don't know why I ever got into this spying business in the first place. Clatter got me started."

Ki hugged her beautiful form hard against him, and a moment later they lay back on the bed.

"Sweet Ki. Make me feel good, the way you did the other time. There's no rush; we have all night. Make me feel safe and wanted and just ever so sexy. The way you make love is wonderful."

Ki did as she asked. Then they slept and made love again, and then sometime later Ki was aware of Sally getting out of bed.

"I have to go down to the outhouse," she said. "Can't stand to use those damn chamber pots."

Ki sat up and watched her dress. "You'll come right back? They might be watching the hotel."

"Don't worry, I'll be back. Another good loving, then I'll be ready to get on that stage. I brought most of my savings with me in my reticule. I never go anywhere without it these days." She picked up the purse and turned to the door.

"You have another nap. I'll be back in five minutes, and we'll find a new way to please each other."

Ki sat on the bed. He knew he shouldn't let her go alone. He should get up and dress and go with her. But before he could get himself out of bed, Sally unlocked the door, waved at him, and hurried out. He heard her lock the door and walk down the hall.

Ki lifted his brows and fell back on the bed. It would be all right. In five minutes Sally would be back. All he had to do was stay awake until she returned.

Even as he thought it, his eyes closed. He popped them open, but they crept shut again. A moment later he slept.

Ki came awake with a start. The sun had chased away the darkness. He looked beside him. Sally wasn't there. Ki sprang out of bed and dressed in record time.

Where should he start to look? It was just past five-thirty and fully light. He checked the outhouse behind the hotel, but it was empty. Her place. He jogged through the street to the apartment over the saloon, but the door was locked. He pounded on it, but no one came.

Ki worked on the back door lock with a piece of wire, and it opened. Sally wasn't in the apartment. It hadn't been disturbed. He ran back to the hotel. She must have met another person she felt safe with. That had to be it.

Ki helped open the small restaurant across from the hotel at six that morning, and by six-thirty the news came: Sally Wondersome had been found murdered on the back porch of the part-time Baptist preacher, Oliver Pierpoint, who was also a miner and a Julian Mining District committeeman.

Marshal Myles Zane wired the county sheriff to get up to Julian by first stage. He'd had three killings in the last twenty-four hours, and he wasn't about to take care of it by himself. Sheriff Nelson wired back within a half hour that he'd be in Julian as quickly as the morning stage could make it.

Town Marshal Zane breathed a sigh of relief and tried to do what he guessed a real lawman would do with three bodies on his hands.

Ki told Jessie about the two fresh murders in the small town as she ate breakfast. She scowled.

"It all ties together, but just how, I don't know," Jessie said as she picked at her food. "Clatter and Maxwell have to be the top suspects in Sally's murder. The gold robber is the suspect in the Wells Fargo detective's death, but we don't know who that is. Somehow everything ties in with Lawson Blaine's killing at the Ready Relief mine. If only we knew who did that, we'd have the key to the whole puzzle."

Sheriff Charles Nelson arrived on a special stage in Julian slightly after two P.M. He talked briefly with Marshal Zane, then arrested Oliver Pierpoint. An hour later, the sheriff released him.

Sheriff Nelson was a tall man with wide shoulders and a considerable belly. He wore two pearl-handled pistols, and some said he'd never fired either one of them. He had on town pants, a white shirt with a string tie, and a fringed buckskin vest. A cigar clamped on the right side of his jaw had not been lighted. He had sent a note to the hotel, and now stared up from the marshal's desk at Ki and Jessie, who stood in front of it.

130

"Yes, Miss Starbuck. Howdy. I met your father once. Terrible about his sudden demise. Understand you're here on another matter, the death of one Lawson Blaine. What interests me more is what you might know about the Wells Fargo detective, Irving Davis."

"We met with him yesterday and talked about the robbery," Jessie said. "He wanted to talk to us because we were at the scene of the wrecked gold-wagon stage and followed the robber's tracks."

"Were you the two who found the pair of dead men near the cabin?"

"Yes, sir," Ki said. "Both shot at close range then dumped in a shallow grave. You've got one gold robber to find now, not three."

"What about the man you took out of the saloon for a chat in the alley yesterday, Ki? Then he was promptly gunned down by rifle rounds."

"I'd like to know who shot him. Miss Starbuck and I think he was the man who hired a pair of bushwhackers who tried to kill us early yesterday. The two attackers were sent to you by the marshal. I didn't kill the man. I don't carry a gun."

"So I've been told." The sheriff struck a match, started to light the cigar, then blew out the match. "So what about the last death, this Sally Wondersome? I understand she was a high-priced fancy woman."

"That's right, Sheriff. I saw her last night. She was terrified. I suggested that she take the morning stage out of town. Looks like she didn't quite make it."

The sheriff's brows lifted. "Did she say why she was terrified, or who she feared?"

"She did. One man's name is J. D. Clatter, the other is Washington Maxwell. Both own mines here. She said she was spying on both of them and getting paid by both. Evidently one of them found out about her double-dealing. Either that or she learned something from one of the men that she shouldn't have known."

"What would be important enough to get her killed?" the sheriff asked.

131

"In this case it might have been facts about a man's murder. Or it could have been information about a sixty-thousand-dollar gold robbery."

The sheriff stood, surprised. "You're suggesting that one of the mine owners might be involved in one or the other of those crimes?"

"Sheriff, we're almost certain that one of them is the villain in this crime spree," Jessie said. "We just don't know which one and we have no proof. We have suspicion, motive, innuendo, and a lot of circumstantial evidence, but nothing we can take to court."

"So you have nothing," the sheriff said. "Too bad. I would have arrested him and had him on his way to San Diego county jail in an hour."

"No evidence yet," Ki said. "But we're getting them both mighty nervous. One of them tried to have us killed yesterday. We almost found out who it was, but the rifle shots killed our chances in that alley."

The sheriff sat down and drew some circles and squares on a pad of paper with a pencil. He looked up. "Would it do me any good to go out to the site of the wrecked stage and dead horses?"

"No," Ki said.

"Probably not the cabin either, where the two men died."

"I don't see how it would help, Sheriff Nelson," Jessie said.

"So what the hell am I supposed to do?" the sheriff asked. "I ain't no damn detective."

"You could visit all eight of the mine owners who shipped gold on that treasure wagon," Ki said. "Include Clatter and Maxwell. Maybe one of them will make a mistake and slip up on something."

"Damned little to go on," the sheriff said.

"They've already made too many mistakes. One more might do them in," Jessie said.

The sheriff scowled. "You two are targets again, you know. From what I hear the two of you got this murder business all started. Maybe you should go on a trip to San Diego until it cools down a little around here."

"We can take care of ourselves, Sheriff Nelson. We won't get in your way. Chances are we just might be able to help a little. Now, there is one more man we want to see."

They wished the lawman well and left the city marshal's office.

"Who are we going to see?" Ki asked.

"Vince Hirlbach. I've got a few more technical questions for him."

Vince was in his office, working on the schematic of a mine showing eight levels, tunnels, shafts, and the location of a stamping mill. He grinned when they came in.

"You guys sure know how to get a town steamed up," he said. "There's been more going on here in the past week than in the past ten years."

"Three bodies in less than twenty-four hours does get people's attention," Jessie said. "I've got some more questions. You have time to talk?"

"Always time for a pretty lady."

"We found another strand for our hangman's rope. Ki talked to Sally last night. She had been spying for both Clatter and Maxwell and reporting to both, playing both ends against the middle. So more evidence that the killer must be one of the two mine owners. Say the killer and the gold robber are the same man. How can he get that stolen gold into circulation?"

"Like we talked about before. It could be melted down and mixed in with his own and stamped with his mine name and a new date."

"What if he didn't want to sell it to the government?"

"There isn't much of a free market for gold. Certainly not large amounts. Jewelers use some, and dentists, but not fifty or sixty pounds."

"So we're back to bleeding it in with the mix of the mine. How long would it take to get all that stolen gold back into the system so it could be sold to the mint?"

"Say Clatter did the deed. Say he had two bricks in the shipment. He wouldn't have to do anything to them. He could have them ready for the next shipment and claim a rich streak. The other bricks would have to be melted down and restamped, maybe one new brick every shipment. Might take a year to work it all into his sales."

"That's what I was afraid of," Jessie said.

Ki stood and walked around the office, his face showing a controlled anger Jessie had seldom seen in him before. "Now I think of a question I should have asked Sally. We were trying to figure out how we could identify the man on that wanted poster. He's got a tattoo on his right shoulder and a bullet scar on his left arm. But how do you take a mine owner's shirt off? Sally took their shirts off enough to have every flaw on their bodies memorized. She could have told us if either of them had the name Rose tattooed on his shoulder."

Jessie shook her head. "We could have known for sure who that wanted poster was for. My money is still riding on the man on that poster as the killer."

"There's another way," Vince said. "Maxwell is well known at both of our local houses that feature soiled doves. I'd bet a dollar and a half that Clatter isn't a stranger there, either. Ki and I could make a quick survey of the ladies before they get to their busy time of day and see what we can find out."

Jessie laughed and nodded. "Why do you guys always get the tough assignments? But I wouldn't think it would take a whole half hour with each girl in the house, would you, Ki?"

Ki grinned. "We'll have to make it more of a social call than business. There must be six or eight girls in each house."

Jessie planted her fists on her hips. "Well, you two, don't just stand there smiling like two cats in a bowl of catnip. Get out of here and do your research, no matter how tough it might be."

★

Chapter 15

Ki walked up to the green door on the whorehouse half a block off Main, which Vince Hirlbach had pointed out.

"That's the most expensive bordello of the two," Vince cautioned. "Might be that the two mine owners would go there more often. Old gal who runs the place uses the name Wanda. She's a scorcher, so watch out for her."

Ki started to knock, then shrugged and turned the doorknob and walked inside. He stood in a parlor with no hall or entryway. It had wallpaper in a fancy pattern, overstuffed furniture with lots of pillows, and a small bar at the far end big enough for only two men to stand at side by side.

Nobody was in the place. Ki coughed once, then looked up the flight of stairs along the far wall.

"Anybody home?" he called. He waited a moment. When no reaction came, he called again. "Anybody here?"

He heard a door slam, and feet slapped along the hallway beyond the end of the second-floor steps.

"You know what in hell time it is?" a gravel voice bellowed from somewhere above. Ki couldn't have said if it was a man or a woman. He heard more sounds of feet or slippers hitting the hallway floor. A moment later a henna-red-haired woman looked over the stair railing.

"You know what the hell time it is?" she brayed. Her hair was tousled and uncombed. She wore a robe that once had been purple.

Ki looked up and grinned. "Somewhere around ten o'clock in the morning, I'd guess," he said.

"Damn right. Middle of sleep time for us working girls. What the hell you want?" She scowled, then pushed forward and looked at him again over the banister. "You that Japo in town stirring things up?"

"Must be me. I need to talk to you and your girls when they get up. When's that?"

"Talk? Talk? My girls don't talk. They get paid for assholes like you poking them. You got a mind to do all seven of my beauties?"

"At two dollars a throw?"

"Two dollars hell. Three dollars for all but one and five for her."

The woman headed down the steps. She was huge, over 250 pounds Ki estimated and not more than five feet tall. She waddled halfway down.

"Talk? What in hell you want to talk about?"

"Do J. D. Clatter and Washington Maxwell ever do business here?"

"Hell yes. Damn near every man in town's been in here one time or another. Clatter is almost a regular. Maxwell used to be. Why them two?"

"I need to know if either one of them has a tattoo."

The woman opened her robe, exposing one ponderous breast and a tattoo of a green-and-purple snake curled around her outsize gland.

"Tattoo? Hell yes, lots of men and some women have them. You like Wanda's little snake?" She laughed and closed her robe. "Why the hell's a man's tattoo so important?"

"Evidence. Miss Starbuck and I are searching for a killer, and the tattoo is evidence. Does either of the two men have a tattoo?"

Wanda paused. She rubbed her fleshy face with one big hand and at last shook her red head of hair. "Damned if I know. I

136

don't see them with their shirts off much anymore. Two of my girls would know. Cost you."

"Both of these girls have slept with Clatter and Maxwell and can tell me if either one or both have tattoos on their upper bodies?"

"If they can't, I'd say my girls didn't earn their pay. Cost you, Japo."

Ki took a five-dollar greenback from his wallet and held it out so she could see it. "A five spot for the information. That's all I want right now."

Wanda frowned, shrugged, and struggled back up the half flight of steps to the hall. She puffed when she made it to the top. "I'll wake them and send them down. Don't expect ravishing beauties this time of day. Take a couple of minutes." She scowled at him for a moment, then waved and vanished down the hall.

Ki sat on a red couch, picked up a magazine, and read part of an article.

Five minutes later he heard someone on the steps. A tall woman with long black hair and wearing a white dressing gown came down the stairs. She was barefoot, and her hair had only been combed enough to keep it in place. Her face was wan and pale and her eyes cautious.

She looked at Ki. "I'm Nellie. You wanted to ask about Clatter and Maxwell?"

Ki stood as the girl came on down the stairs. She stopped in front of him. She was taller than he had expected.

He took her hand and shook it once, then released it. "Yes. Do you know the two men?"

"I know Clatter best. Haven't been with Maxwell for, oh, a year now I guess. He always asks for Priscilla."

"Does Clatter have a tattoo?"

Nellie shook her head. "I'm almost sure that he doesn't. Unless he has a small one hidden somewhere."

"No name tattooed on his arms or shoulders?"

"No, I'm certain of that. I can't remember much about Maxwell. After a while I don't even look at the customers."

"Thanks, Nellie, you've been a help to me. I'm eliminating suspects. Oh, please don't say anything about this to anyone."

Nellie nodded and walked back up the steps.

Wanda appeared at the top of the stairs a moment later.

"Hey, Japo. Priscilla is the other one to see, but she ain't feeling none too good. She had a rough night. You come back about four this afternoon, and she'll talk to you then. Just leave the fiver on the couch. I'll pick it up when I come down."

She turned, then looked back. "Oh, twist that damn night lock on the door when you go out. I don't want nobody else busting in here in the middle of the night."

When he walked outside, Ki found Vince waiting for him. He grinned.

"Well, what do you think of our Wanda? Isn't she a beauty? Lots of padding there to keep a man from injuring himself in the heat of passion."

Ki chuckled. "Lots of padding. But not enough information. I found one girl who knew Clatter. She said he absolutely had no tattoo on his arms or shoulders or anywhere else."

"What about Maxwell?"

"The girl who knows him best is Priscilla, and she isn't feeling well this morning. Middle of the night for them. I go back at four this afternoon to talk."

"At least we've eliminated one suspect. Does that narrow it down to Maxwell?"

Ki shook his head. "I don't know. Seems he's our best killer, but we still have no evidence. The sheriff won't arrest anyone without strong proof of guilt. We still have to get something he can take to court."

"I struck out," Vince said. "Miz Crawford said she hadn't seen either man in her place for at least a year. None of the girls who were with her then are still there now. A big turnover in whores in this business from what I understand."

"No personal knowledge of the personnel?" Ki asked.

"Not really my kind of woman," Vince said. "Fact is, I have this little rule about never paying for love, if you don't count a fancy dinner and a bottle of wine or two. So far, so good."

They walked back to Main Street, stopped by Vince's office, and then went on toward the hotel. They found Jessie on the boardwalk coming toward them.

138

"Good news!" she said as soon as she saw them. She waved them to the front of a store and took a folded paper from her reticule.

"The widow Blaine did some more looking around her dearly departed husband's things and found the wanted poster from Rock Springs."

Jessie unfolded it and pushed it against the wall. There was a big headline offering two thousand dollars for a man dead or alive, then a description and a line engraving of a man's face. It was small and not clear.

"Can you make out who it is?" Jessie asked.

Ki took a better look, held it so the sun hit it and studied it, then shook his head. "I can't figure if it's either one of our suspects."

Jessie frowned and brushed long coppery blond hair out of her face. "Neither can I. It could be either Clatter or Maxwell. I was hoping this would be a clincher."

She lifted her brows in resignation. "So what did you two find out with our friendly soiled doves?"

"I have a guarantee that Clatter isn't our tattooed man," Ki said. "Nellie says definitely he has no tattoos on his arms or shoulders."

"What about Maxwell?"

"I can't talk to Priscilla, the girl who knows Maxwell best, until four this afternoon. She had a tough night of work. At least we have one less prime suspect."

"But nothing we can take to the judge. The poster says the tattoo is red and green and is the name 'Rose.' Let's hope Priscilla has a good memory."

"Even so, we won't have the evidence we need," Ki said.

"Maybe we have to pressure the killer again. This wanted poster put up on a bulletin board somewhere might get some results."

Ki read from the wanted. "This guy pulled a bank robbery and got away with the railroad payroll, over twenty thousand dollars' worth. He killed his two accomplices and vanished."

"Great humanitarian," Vince said. "It's the same pattern as the two gold-train robbers here who were shot down."

Vince read the poster again. "Travis G. Young is the name the robber used in Wyoming. We might call Maxwell by that name and see if he reacts."

"He's had too much time under his new name," Jessie said. "Let's tack up the wanted poster on the Tall Saloon bulletin board and then send unsigned notes to both Maxwell and Clatter saying that there's a note on the bulletin board they should be interested in."

Vince bobbed his head. "Yes, it should work. I'll write up the notes and find somebody to deliver them so Maxwell won't know they came from either of you."

Jessie doubled up one fist and put it on her hip, then nodded. "Yes, Vince, the sooner the better. See if a rider can get to both places before noon. I'm going back to talk to the sheriff. There must be something he can do to move this along a little faster. If he can't help, I might be sending some telegrams to Wells Fargo. I have another idea."

Vince touched Jessie's shoulder and hurried toward his office. Ki looked at her.

"What idea?" he asked.

"First we tie up everything we can on Maxwell. If we can catch him in the act, we won't have to prove the other robbery."

"Another gold wagon run?"

"That's the idea. I don't think a visit to the sheriff would help right now. Let's send a wire to Wells Fargo headquarters in San Francisco with the idea. Give them a day to think it over."

They sent the wire, suggesting the idea of using a fortified gold wagon with special guards inside and out and sending it out during the day so it would be harder to surprise.

They met Vince for lunch at Mama's Cafe.

"The notes are on their way and should be delivered about now," Vince said. "You put the wanted poster up?"

"Right in the middle of the bulletin board," Ki said. "Now all we have to do is watch for a reaction."

After a quick lunch, the three of them stood at the window in Vince's office and watched the bulletin board at the Tall Saloon across the street.

It seemed that half the people in town stopped to read notices there this noon. It was almost one o'clock before Vince spotted Clatter striding up the street.

"Here he comes and he looks worried," Vince said.

They watched the man crowd two others aside to read the notices. He wasn't attracted to the wanted poster.

"Looks like he's reading every announcement there," Jessie said.

"He read the wanted and passed it over like it was yesterday's news," Ki said.

They watched as the mine owner read the board from one side to the other, then went back over them again. When he finished scouring the papers for the second time, Clatter shrugged and walked back toward his mine.

"If that was me on that wanted poster, I'd get it out of sight as soon as I could," Vince said.

The other two agreed with him, and they brought up chairs for a longer wait.

Less than twenty minutes later, a rider pulled to a stop outside the saloon and tied up. The man was Maxwell. He went directly to the bulletin board and stared at the wanted poster. He looked at nothing else. In one swift move he ripped the notice off the board, folded it, and put it inside his shirt.

Maxwell marched back to his horse, mounted, and rode away toward the Ready Relief mine.

Jessie smiled.

"Looks like we've found our poster boy," Vince said.

"Proof," Ki said softly. "We still don't have any proof."

"The tattoo will help," Vince said.

Ki stood and headed for the door. "I'll get over to my favorite bawdy house. Maybe Priscilla is feeling better by now."

Jessie stood as well. "I'm going to talk to the manager of the Wells Fargo office here. If San Francisco won't authorize a real gold shipment, we'll fake one and hope to get Maxwell excited enough to attack."

Ki hurried out the front door.

Vince moved over beside Jessie. He caught her chin and tipped it up and kissed her lips hungrily. When he broke off the kiss, Jessie opened her eyes and stared up at him.

"Mr. Hirlbach. You know that is not the way to put me in the best frame of mind to negotiate with Wells Fargo."

"Wasn't worried about Wells Fargo," Vince said. "Just taking advantage of a beautiful woman when I have the chance."

Jessie reached up, pulled his face down to hers, and kissed him again. She nibbled at his lips, then met his open mouth and sighed in delight.

When the kiss ended, he held her tightly against his chest and kissed her forehead. "Now I know why I always wanted a couch in my office," he said.

Jessie made noises deep in her throat but pushed back from him. "Maybe we could have supper tonight and then go up to my room."

"Done, a contract. Dinner at six in the hotel." He let go of her and walked away. When he turned, it was with a sheepish grin. "You know I'm not going to be good for much work myself the rest of the afternoon."

"Good," Jessie said, smiling. "It's fine to know I can affect you that way." She went to him, reached up, and pecked a quick kiss on his lips. "Now, I want to have a long talk with the Wells Fargo manager."

Q. L. Laporte hoisted out of his chair in the Wells Fargo office and shook hands with Jessie.

"Want to thank you and your friend for what you told the sheriff about the gold robbery," Laporte said. "As you know, we ain't got much law in this place yet. It might be coming soon now with the sheriff's visit. What can I do for you?"

Jessie told him her plan to smoke out the gold robbers.

"Risk another gold shipment so soon?"

"The way I see it, Mr. Laporte, is that the robber is getting nervous by now and is about ready to cut and run. If he does, we'll never prove anything against him. Now is our chance to catch him in the act. I sent San Francisco headquarters a wire this morning urging them to try this plan."

"Well, if they say to go ahead, we go ahead. You mentioned something about putting steel plates in the sides of the coach to protect the guards?"

For the next half hour, Jessie spelled out ways they could protect the guards and the driver. The driver wouldn't be on the high seat. Rather they would cut a hole in the front of the coach roof so the driver could stand in the passenger compartment and still drive.

Laporte looked up and nodded. "It all sounds reasonable, and exciting. I just wonder how many bricks we could get to ship at this early date. I know some of the owners hold back bricks so they won't risk too much at one time."

"Let's see how we could put in some armor to protect the men inside the coach," Jessie said.

They went out back to a spare coach and looked it over. It wasn't one of the big Concords that had prowled the West for so long.

"We can figure out what to do if we get a go-ahead, but I can't alter the coach," Laporte said.

"This rig hasn't been used for a long time," Jessie said.

"Actually it's a discard. The company tried to sell it but couldn't find a buyer."

Jessie looked it over a minute, then nodded. "How much?"

"Company said two hundred dollars. Worth a lot more, but right now things are sort of slow."

"Sold," Jessie said. "I'll make out a bank draft as soon as I get back to the hotel. Meantime I'll get over to the blacksmith and see if he has any sheets of steel or thin sheets of cast iron I can buy. We'll put them on both sides and front and back. Make this box into a fort.

"Mr. Laporte, if you have a stable hand, I'd appreciate some help. We need to get this rig into rolling condition. All four axles need greasing, and we need to give it a good once-over. No idea how far we'll have to pull it before the robbers make a try at the gold."

Laporte stopped her with a wave of his hand. "Miss Starbuck. I know your reputation and your resources. But I'm not even sure that San Francisco will authorize another gold shipment so soon. Now that Irving Davis has been gunned down, they'll want to investigate it all carefully before they ship any more gold."

"I figured that, Mr. Laporte. That's mostly why I bought this rig. If we don't get a go-ahead from San Francisco, we'll set up a phony gold run and fool the robbers. I know this is our only

143

chance to smoke out the killer. He's smart. We don't have any proof, any witnesses. It's this or give up. I never give up."

Laporte watched the woman carefully. Jessie hoped that he saw the hard glint in her eye. She would do this one her way, whether he wanted her to or not.

At last he nodded. "Okay. I see your point. You have a suspect?"

She told him, and Laporte sucked in a breath in surprise.

"Maxwell's one of the big men in this town."

"Anyone can be big when he starts out with twenty thousand in stolen gold. Now let's get to work making this coach into a fort, a gold-wagon fort that we know will do the job."

★

Chapter 16

Jessie talked with Karl Imhoff, the blacksmith in town, and he said he had something she might like. He showed her some steel plates that one of the mine operators had ordered and never come for. Some were four feet long, some five feet, and all a yard wide.

"Would a .45 round go through there?" Jessie asked.

Imhoff shook his head. "Don't know, but reckon we can find out." He went into his shop and came back a moment later with a six-gun. He warned Jessie back and fired at the steel plate, which he had stood on the side and leaned against a tree. The .45 slug hit the plate, flattened, and then dropped to the ground. It had only made a dent in the steel.

"I want four of them," Jessie said. "Two five-footers and two of the four." Imhoff said he'd deliver them to the Wells Fargo stable area within an hour. All he had to do was hook up his horse to his wagon and tote them over there.

Back at the Wells Fargo office, Jessie met Laporte, who came to the rear lot waving a yellow paper at her.

"Afraid I've got some bad news," Laporte said. "My regional manager in San Francisco says I'm not to do anything here until the home office sends in another investigator to check on the loss of the gold and the murder of Irving Davis. They mention your telegram and say under no circumstances should I authorize any kind of a gold shipment until their new investigator has checked out all aspects of the situation."

Jessie nodded. "I figured that's about what they'd say. That's why I bought the coach." She told him about the steel plates.

"But, Miss Starbuck. Don't you see? There's no chance I can help you now. If I do, they'll fire me for sure, and I really need this job. I don't want to dig in the mines anymore."

Jessie touched the man's shoulder. "Mr. Laporte, this isn't something you need to worry about. I'd never do anything that would jeopardize your position here. The company will be glad you sold the old coach. What I do with it is my business."

"But how can you have a gold shipment to attract the robber without any gold? I can't give you any company forms, and certainly no guarantee vouchers for the gold or the usual forms and bills of lading."

"There's an easy way around that, Mr. Laporte. I know who the killer and gold wagon robber is. He's the only one I have to fool. When the wagon gets to his place, the driver simply tells him that new company regulations limit the amount of gold that can be shipped on any one trip to ten gold bricks, and that we're full to the limit. You'll come to his place first for the next run.

"That should fool Maxwell, let him know we have ten gold bricks already and entice him to come after them. We just have to hire a driver for the pickup at the Ready Relief. Be more than happy if you want to do that for us. Then we'll change to Ki as the driver for the actual run out of town."

Laporte grinned his response. "Yeah, I see what you mean about only having to fool Maxwell. I'll be more than glad to be the driver on the pickup. I owe it to my three dead employees to get this cleaned up as fast as possible."

Ki wandered in and looked over the coach. He had guessed where Jessie would be.

"Did you find Priscilla?"

"Did that. She said absolutely that Maxwell has the name 'Rose' tattooed on his right shoulder. He's got to be our killer."

146

Ki borrowed a hammer, a saw, and a wrecking bar and worked on the coach roof, where the driver usually sat. He took off the driver's seat and checked the roof. The front part was directly over the front seat in the coach below.

All he had to do was remove three of the planks in the roof and put a wooden box below on the passenger's seat, and a man could stand on the box with his head barely above the roof line, drive a team of six, and yet make a small target for a bushwhacker.

Ki told Jessie what he proposed to do, and she set him to work. The wagon arrived from the blacksmith, and the two men tugged the heavy sheets of steel off it and leaned them against the coach's rear wheels.

The stable hand had greased all four of the rig's axles and wheels and the tongue, checked the singletrees, and made sure that the brake lever was operating and that the brake shoe was ready to push hard against the steel rim of the right front wooden spoked wheel.

It took Ki an hour and a half to get the planks off the roof of the coach and a proper size of wooden box nailed to the front seat. He stood on it and could see well enough to drive the rig, even though his head barely cleared the top of the roof.

"Now, let's see about getting those armor plates inside the rig," Jessie said.

Laporte brought two more men to help them lift the plates and maneuver the heavy load through the small coach door and inside. The five-foot-long plates were the right size to sit on the passenger seats front and back. The three-foot width of the plates rose well over the open windows and door window, but they would have the leather curtains down to hide them.

Next they worked in the four-foot-long plates, putting one crossways on the front seat and one on the rear. They had to gouge into the upholstery to make them fit. When the two were in place they hoisted in the third one, a five-footer for the side.

Ki went to work inside, building a square framework of two-by-four lumber, which he anchored at the top and bottom of the steel, to hold the plates in position.

Entry into the rig would be obtained by crawling over a plate through a window. With the steel in place and the leather curtains down on the door and windows, there was no sign that the rig was armored.

"The driver standing inside will be a tip-off," Ki said. "I'll fix the planks so we can have them in and the driver's seat in place while we stop by at the Ready Relief. Then when we get back here, we'll pitch the driver's seat aside and I'll drop down in the coach to stand up and drive from there."

Jessie grinned. "Who said you were going to be the driver?"

Ki closed his eyes and made a barely proper bow. "I only assumed that I would be the driver. That decision is yours." He grinned. "Jessie, you can drive it if you want to."

"I might," Jessie said. She looked at Laporte. "How many horses do you usually have on this run, four or six?"

"Six, through the mountains."

"Can six haul this heavy rig?"

"Let's find out."

The stable hand and Ki hitched up a team of six, and the hand sat on the restored driver's seat and drove the rig out to the street, down a block, and back to the rear lot of the Wells Fargo office.

"Drives like a fully loaded rig with about twelve passengers," the stable hand said.

"Can we carry me and three more men inside with rifles?" Ki asked.

Laporte nodded. "That shouldn't be any problem. You figure you won't have to go more than five miles out of town?"

"Right," Jessie said. "Which road has the least brush and trees along it, and the safest route with no sudden drop-offs?"

"That would be the West road to Ramona and then south to San Diego. It's damn near clear-cut out four or five miles."

"When should we do this?" Jessie asked.

"It's always a surprise," Laporte said. "Usually we give the mine owner a seven-hour notice."

It was a little after three in the afternoon by Jessie's small pocket watch. "Let's do it tonight. Mr. Laporte, would you ride out and notify Maxwell at Ready Relief that the next gold wagon run will be tonight, as usual about midnight?"

148

She pretended to slap him, then became serious. "Vince, you know I can't stay here. Just too much to get done in too many places. Afraid I wouldn't be much good at gold mining, but it's been a great few days here with you."

She lay down on top of him, with one breast nuzzling at his mouth.

"Once more. Something different this time. Then I'm going to have to get ready for tomorrow. Honest, as I told you in the cafe, I need a good night's sleep."

An hour later, when Vince had dressed and sat on the bed beside her, he caressed her bare breasts and bent and kissed both. Then he stood.

"Damn, wish I could figure out a way to get you to stay here without kidnapping you and tying you to my bedpost."

"We'll meet again. Let me know where you move. I can often use a good mining engineer."

"I'll do that. I have your Texas address." He kissed her lips once more, then growled, and walked to the door. He cracked it open, saw two people going down the hall, and closed the door softly. The next time he looked out the hall was clear. He winked at Jessie, slipped out, and hurried down the hall.

Jessie smiled remembering the evening. She consulted her small pocket watch. Nearly ten o'clock. She stepped out of bed and laid out her riding clothes: cut-down denims, shirt, her flat-crowned hat, boots, and her gunbelt. With any luck they would have this problem all wrapped up by morning.

As she thought about Washington Maxwell, she knew that he wasn't the kind of a man to go down quick or easy. Even if they stopped a robbery of the wagon, they would have a tough job getting him to come in for a trial. Jessie figured Maxwell was the kind of man who would do almost anything rather than be caught and brought to justice in the courts. That alone worried her.

At eleven o'clock she rapped on the locked outside door of the Wells Fargo office. It opened at once, and Ki greeted her.

"Everything's set. Maxwell expects to roll the rig soon. We have the three riflemen, and I've briefed them about this being a phony gold run, so they won't wonder where the yellow stuff is. They know they could get hurt or killed in this run, and all have signed up with that in mind."

"What about Mr. Laporte?"

"He's out back getting the guards settled down in the hay-mow. We'll pick them up here when we come back. I'll ride inside the coach on the run out to the Ready Relief just in case there's any problem."

Laporte came in the back door and welcomed Jessie.

"This damn better work or I could get my tail feathers singed," Laporte said.

"True, but no risk, no heroes," Jessie said. "If it works, you reclaim the company's sixty thousand in gold and nail the outlaw and the man who killed your Wells Fargo investigator at the same time. That could mean a promotion."

"Maybe. Time we get going. Everything else is set."

Jessie watched the wagon roll down the street. This was nervous time for her. There was nothing she could do but sit and wait. She went back into the Wells Fargo office and thought through it all again. They had done everything they could to be ready. The three rifle guards were in the barn out back, waiting for the rig to return.

They would drive the coach out of the back lot ten minutes before daylight. Any ambushers would be far ahead some-where waiting for them. At least that's the way Jessie would set it up. She stood and went out to the barn and checked the three horses. All were ready, saddled, girths tightened, spare ammo in the saddlebags, and each with a rifle in its boot.

She went back inside and waited. They figured it would take about an hour to get to the Ready Relief and a few minutes to tell Maxwell about the new regulations and that they were filled up for this run. Then about an hour to get back.

Jessie sat in a chair in the office and put her boots up on the desk, and before she knew it, she had dropped off to sleep.

The jangle of harness awoke her. She pulled down her feet and scurried out the back door. The rig sat where it had left from two hours before.

Laporte jumped down from the high seat grinning in the darkness.

"Maxwell swallowed the whole thing like a trout taking a grasshopper," he said.

Ki crawled out of the side window and seconded the motion. "Far as I could tell he wasn't a bit surprised by any of it. He said he figured there would be some new rules. Said he could live by them, but on the next run he wanted to be the first pickup so he could be sure to get his gold to market."

"So, we've got the seed planted," Laporte said. "Wish we'd left somebody behind on the trail back to town to see what Maxwell did."

Ki eased the *tanto* in and out of his scabbard. "Guess we'll find out in a few hours."

"We leave at five A.M. sharp," Laporte said. "Leastwise Ki and the three guards and the wagon do. We can leave the horses hitched for a time. They can sleep standing up if they want to. As for me, I want to catch a few winks."

They all took catnaps on a couch in the office and in chairs. Ki slept on the floor.

At four-thirty they were up and moving. Laporte had already checked the harness and the coach. All was set. He kicked the riflemen guards out of the hay and got them inside the rig. Then Ki slipped down the hole in the top of the roof and caught the reins.

The stagecoach left five minutes early. Laporte, Jessie, and a spare horse tied behind Jessie's mount left thirty minutes after the wagon. They kept their pace at a slow walk.

"About right," Laporte said. "We don't want to run up too close to the rig and give it away."

By the time they hit the edge of town, the sun was rimming the ridges far to the east. It brought some warmth to the high country.

An hour later they were four miles out of town on a slight downgrade through a pleasant valley. They would do a lot of downhill if they had to go much farther. From time to time on open stretches, they could see the gold wagon ahead of them. When this happened, they slowed down.

"When will they attack?" Jessie asked.

Laporte looked ahead. "Rig should be about coming into a patch of woods with a trail through it. Be a good spot for an

153

ambush. A few shadows in there even at high noon."

Just after he spoke, they heard three rifle shots from ahead. They spurred their mounts forward. Jessie pulled the repeating Winchester from the boot and cranked a round into the chamber. She saw that Laporte had done the same.

They moved down a slight slope, across a small valley, and then up into the edge of a rise with trees all over it.

More rifle shots came then, some measured in pace, others in rapid-fire order.

Another quarter mile, and they rode to the edge of the woods and plunged in. They slowed as the sound of the rifles came closer.

Jessie pulled up. "Over there," she said. She pointed to the small cloud of white smoke in some light timber fifty yards from the road. They both jumped off their mounts, left the reins down to ground-tie the animals, and scurried behind trees.

Jessie and Laporte both fired at the base of the puffs of white smoke they saw in the brush and trees to the left of the trail. Jessie emptied her weapon, filled the chamber, and fired six more rounds before she realized no more smoke was coming from the brush they had targeted.

They ran forward from cover to cover, making the small trees work for them. A hundred yards ahead they came around a small turn in the trail, and then they could see the wagon. It had stopped. Jessie could see one of the horses down and not moving.

No more shots came from the wagon.

"Go back for the horses," Jessie shouted at Laporte. He nodded and ran back the way they had come.

She rushed on to the fake gold wagon. "Ki, are you still in there?" Jessie bellowed from thirty yards away and from behind a Jeffrey pine tree. She didn't want to be shot by friendly forces.

Ki kicked his feet out the side window away from where the gunfire had originated and dropped off the wagon.

Jessie ran up.

"Anybody hurt?"

"Just two horses. That steel did a great job on those rifle rounds."

154

"We've got our mounts coming. Get the guards out of there. Tell them to cut the dead horses out of the harness and take this rig back to town. We've got some tracking to do."

Five minutes later, Laporte had the horses up, and he, Jessie, and Ki rode toward the spot from where the bushwhackers had made their attack. They found it easily enough: trampled-down grass, a log to fire over, and the remains of sandwiches and three abandoned paper sacks. Back twenty yards they found a place where three horses had been tied for some time.

Ki swept the area and soon picked up the tracks.

"Three horses, all laden about the same, moving out to the east. My bet is that they head for the stage road."

Fifty yards up the trail they found one of the horses. It had been hit by a rifle round and could walk on only three legs. Ki held the rifle Jessie gave him to the horse's head and put the animal out of its misery.

"One horse is double loaded. That will slow them down," Ki said.

Another hundred yards ahead they took two rounds of rifle fire. All three ducked and kicked their mounts into the brush. Ki came off his horse, left the rifle in the boot, and sprinted into the brush toward the place where the shots had been fired from.

Jessie looked at Laporte. "You better go back and tend to the coach and horses. I'll pay for the dead ones. Get the coach back to town. This is Ki's specialty out here. We'll see you back in town."

She waited two minutes, caught Ki's horse, and nudged her mount ahead. She came out of some brush and faced a hundred-yard crossing of open ground. Halfway over she saw a man on the ground. He wasn't moving. Jessie charged ahead with her face near the mount's mane. She stopped at the body, but it wasn't Ki. The corpse had a shiny silver star buried halfway in the side of its neck and was covered with blood.

Jessie galloped on into the fringe of brush ahead, leading Ki's mount. One down, two to go. Jessie heard gunfire ahead, then silence. She kept her rifle ready, now with a full load, and worked forward at a walk.

Ki and the two robbers had to be up there somewhere. The problem was where were they, and would they see her before she saw them?

★

Chapter 17

Three rifle shots jolted close together into the mountain stillness. Jessie ducked automatically, but then realized that the rounds had not come toward her. They had sounded not too far ahead. She dropped off her horse, ground-tied her, and sprinted ten yards forward, to a two-foot-thick pine tree.

She was in a pine woods now, with almost no underbrush and medium-size Jeffrey pines growing every twenty or thirty feet. From behind a tree she could see a haze of white smoke forty yards ahead. She saw no horses.

Jessie settled on her stomach behind a pine and worked around to the side for a shot. She aimed at a suspect tree, then came away from the sights and watched it with both eyes. Something moved to the right side. Then a small movement to the left. She sighted in again on the right side, refined her aim, and fired.

A scream of protest came from a man ahead. He bellowed in rage and stood with his hands in the air.

"I give up, dammit. Quit shooting!" Only a second after the man's words ended, two shots blasted from beyond the robber and he jolted forward with hot lead in his back. He hit the mulched forest floor and didn't move.

Ki spurted from one tree to another twenty yards into the

forest. A shot slashed through the air but missed him. Jessie pumped three rounds into the haze of telltale black powder smoke well back in the trees. In the covering fire, Ki moved forward two more trees. He turned and waved at her.

She put three more rounds into the same area as the first ones, and again Ki sprinted from tree to tree, until he was past the open country and back to more underbrush that concealed him. In a moment Ki vanished.

Jessie thought about it a bit, then raced back for the horses. She led Ki's and rode around the side of the open area, then plunged into the underbrush near where she had lost Ki.

She saw the second robber, who still lay on the ground. Jessie figured he was dead or would be soon. Shot down by the man who had hired him. It followed Maxwell's pattern.

Jessie stopped and listened. Far ahead she heard a horse, then a second one. She galloped through the light brush, heading for the horse talk. Halfway there she saw Ki step out from a tree and hold up one hand.

She slowed and let go of Ki's horse's reins. Ki sprang on board the mount, and they were riding.

"Just one man left," Ki said. "I haven't had a good look at him, but I'd bet half the ranch he's Maxwell. He got to his horse." They rode hard through the brush. "Whoever he is, I hit him with a star in the leg. He's bleeding and hurting, but he's still a good shot. He hit my sleeve back there."

They burst out of the brush into the open pine forest again. A forest fire a dozen years before had denuded the light brush, and now only the sturdy pines that had been far above the flames survived.

A third of the way across they saw a rider. He turned and fired a shot at them. Ki took the rifle from his boot and fired twice. He stopped his horse. With the mount halted, Ki fired twice more, and the animal ahead screamed in pain and fury and went down. The man aboard fell to the ground and was slow getting up, and Ki's last shot missed him by inches. He rolled behind a tree.

"Ride!" Ki thundered. They galloped ahead through the open woods, then veered to the left for more tree protection as a shot came too close.

In the trees, Ki slid off his mount. "Don't get too near him," he said and rushed forward, using the trees for cover. Jessie turned sharply. Now she could get behind the robber. She rode hard through the trees, then circled around the spot where she figured the shooter must be lying. He could play dead, wait for his chance, and gun down Ki.

Jessie wondered if she had gone far enough. She paused and listened. Somewhere ahead of her, back the direction she had come, she heard a single rifle shot. Maybe the man was running low on ammo.

Jessie filled the magazine on her repeater, tied her mount, and slid off. She moved toward the rifle shot slowly, watching with all of her concentration forward for any sign of movement, trying to hear any noise.

She moved ten yards and paused beside a two-foot pine.

No sound. No movement ahead.

Jessie worked forward again, careful not to make a sound. She put a foot down only when she was sure it was safe from breaking a branch or making any noise.

Twenty feet farther on, she slid behind another Jeffrey pine and edged around from ground level to look ahead. A man stepped from behind a tree, but she didn't see him until he moved toward her. He was only twenty feet away and looking back the way he had come. Jessie lifted her rifle and aimed at his chest. She saw his face. Maxwell!

"Hold it, Maxwell, the game is over. Your killing days are done."

He looked up, surprised, then saw her hidden partly behind the tree. He lifted his rifle and pulled the trigger. The firing pin hit an empty chamber. Jessie had tensed; now her finger tightened on the trigger.

"Kneel down and put your hands on your head," Jessie barked.

Maxwell laughed. "Go ahead and shoot me. You can't. No woman can kill me. Hell, give it a try. I'm getting out of here."

His right leg showed blood from thigh to boot top. He walked with a limp. Jessie lowered her sights to his legs and pulled the trigger. Nothing happened.

She stared at her rifle. The breech wasn't closed. A round had jammed halfway into the firing slot. Maxwell ran to the left.

Jessie screeched in anger and drew her six-gun, but by then Maxwell was out of sight in the heavier brush.

"Ki, up this way," Jessie yelled. "He's on foot and out of rounds."

Jessie raced back to where she had left her horse and galloped to the spot where Ki stood reading sign. He turned and followed the killer into the brush. Jessie rode ahead and, to her surprise, in another thirty yards came out on the West road. A young cowboy sat in the middle of the road holding his right arm.

She rode up to him. "What happened?" Jessie asked.

"Some crazy man with blood all over his leg threatened me with a knife and took my horse, then broke my arm over his knee and rode away laughing."

Ki burst out of the brush on his horse. He took in the scene in a second and waved down the road.

"Follow those tracks," he said, and they rode east toward Julian, reading the horse's fresh tracks.

"He was Maxwell?" Ki asked.

"Yes. I was twenty feet from him and my rifle jammed." She handed it to Ki, who worked on it as they rode.

"He has a head start, so he'll beat us back to town," Jessie said. "Where will we go, his townhouse or the mine?"

"The mine. That's where he'll have the stolen gold. He'll want that and all he's taken from his partners."

They punished the horses and made it to town in twenty minutes. They paused at the livery only long enough to get two fresh mounts, another rifle, and more ammunition, then rode at a canter out to the Ready Relief mine.

The manager met them at the office door.

"What the hell is going on? Mr. Maxwell just rode in half-covered with blood. He demanded that I bandage his leg and get water and food packed for a trip."

"Is he gone?" Jessie asked.

"Yes. He took a packhorse into the smeltering shed and was there for ten minutes, then he came out, grabbed the flour sack

160

of food and water, and headed out east riding one horse and trailing another one with the food sack tied on her. Nothing out there but the desert for fifty miles."

Ki found the tracks coming out of the smeltering-shed door. Sure enough, two horses heading east. Within ten yards the tracks showed that the mounts were galloping, still heading east.

They walked their horses as Ki read the trail. It headed generally toward the Banner Grade wagon road that wound down to the desert.

"Where can he hide down there?" Jessie asked.

Ki shook his head. "Maybe he plans on riding all the way through to the first town, wherever that is."

"We've got the tables turned on him," Jessie said. "Now he's riding heavy and we're light. We should be able to catch him. If he hits the Banner Grade road, we'll push these horses."

Fifteen minutes later the tracks of the two horses entered the Banner Grade trail, and the chasers lifted their mounts to a gentle canter down the slants of the wagon road.

A half hour at that pace brought them nearly to the bottom of the trail, and they entered the strange world of the middle desert. It was what the old-timers called a three-inch desert, where the annual rainfall amounted to three inches, and much of that came in two or three crashing, boiling, wind-driven thunderstorms.

Lots of sagebrush and smaller desert plants dotted the area. In the washes a few larger trees grew, and everywhere there were cactus of a dozen different varieties, including the ocotillo, which looked like a giant upside-down octopus with thorns. At the bottom of the trail they found a small community where the creek came out of the mountains. It had spawned a ten-acre glen of trees, bush, and grass. Downstream the water soon was swallowed up by the desert.

At Banner there was one store and two houses, all near the stream, which was a life giver to those coming in from the desert and those heading into it.

Here and there traffic had blotted out the fugitive's tracks, but they found where Maxwell had paused by the stream to

161

refill his canteens and water his horses. Then the trail plunged on forward into the heart of the desert floor.

"Where is he going?" Jessie asked again.

"Maybe he wants to bury all his gold out here and then give up," Ki suggested. "What could we charge him with, besides attacking an empty stagecoach?"

"Rock Springs still wants him," Jessie said. "Somehow I don't expect they'll ever see him again, under any name."

About five miles from Banner, a crude sign pointed south and said "Valicitos Stage Station."

The stage road was only a lonesome track through the sand and rocks and around an occasional smoke tree. The area looked like one huge dry lake that extended for miles. It was as flat as the inside of a fry pan.

"I thought we were gaining on him," Ki said. "But where the hell is he?"

Before the sounds of the words had died in the harsh desert air, a rifle shot blasted from the right and a bullet slapped through the air between the two riders. They bailed off their mounts and put the animals between the rifle and themselves.

"Over there behind some sage," Ki said. "There must be a small runoff gully."

"You go right, I'll go left," Jessie said. They walked their mounts, crouching behind them for cover. Jessie took one more rifle round that missed; then the gunman remained quiet.

Jessie soon reached a spot where she could see down the length of the now-dry streambed. A horse lay in the wash, with only an occasional pawing of one foot.

For a while she couldn't see the man. Then she found him lying on the bank of the wash. He sat up and swung a canteen at something, then screamed. Jessie rode forward quickly. She hadn't spotted Maxwell's rifle, so she kept on the watch. She saw Ki coming from the other side.

She was fifty feet away when she realized what had happened. Maxwell had tried to take a shortcut off the trail and blundered into a colony of rattlesnake burrows. As she came closer she saw that the bottom of the wash was writhing with hundreds, perhaps thousands, of snakes.

162

Rattlers often congregated in one place and formed themselves into huge balls and coils. They used small caves or washes where other animals had dug into the soft side of the earth. Once they were disturbed, the whole ball came apart, and every snake that could struck at the intruder.

The horse was down in the midst of them and must have been bitten hundreds of times on all four legs before the venom had reached the big quadruped's heart and it had gone down. Now the snakes struck repeatedly at the downed animal.

Jessie couldn't figure out if Maxwell had crawled out of the wash or if he'd dismounted first. Either way there were now dozens of snakes around him. By the time Jessie was within thirty feet of the man, she saw two rattlers hanging on his arm by their fangs. A dozen had coiled near him and were striking him whenever he moved.

Where was the other horse? She saw it with packs tied on its back, wandering fifty yards away, looking for grass. It found none.

Ki rode up closer and called to Maxwell. The man turned, his eyes glazed as he tried to focus.

"Help me," he said, his words slurred, soft.

"Can you walk?" Jessie called.

Maxwell shook his head.

"Don't go in there," Jessie called to Ki. "Nothing we can do will help him now. Even if we roped him and dragged him out of there, he's taken too many strikes by now." As she spoke, Jessie saw three more rattlers strike, plant their venom, and pull back ready to strike again.

"Maxwell, you stole the gold?" Jessie asked.

"Yes!" the word came as a defiant admission.

"You killed the two men who helped you and buried them at the cabin?"

"Yes, yes. Now get me out of here."

Ki slid down from his horse, gathered a handful of long-dead grass and some dead cactus stems, and lit them on fire. With the torch he moved slowly toward the doomed man. The snakes rushed away from the flames. Jessie made a second torch and handed it to Ki, who pushed back the rattlers. He touched

163

fire to those hanging onto the man, and they came loose and slithered away.

After five minutes of torching the ground around Maxwell, Ki had a pathway cleared, and he caught the killer under the arms and pulled him well away from the snakes.

Maxwell lay on his side, his eyes away from the sun.

"Maxwell, did you rob the bank in Rock Springs, Wyoming?" Jessie asked.

"Yes. They can't hurt me now. Nobody can. Is it night already? Seems like a short day."

Ki looked at Jessie, shook his head, and held up his hand, showing five fingers. She figured he meant Maxwell had no more than five minutes to live.

"What about Lawson Blaine, Maxwell?" Jessie asked. "Why did you kill him?"

Maxwell tried to look at her, but he saw only darkness. "Lawson, good man. Liked him. But he heard me planning the gold robbery with one of the men who helped me. We couldn't let him live to expose the plot. He had to die."

The words tumbled out, his speech clear for a moment.

"The same with Sally Wondersome," Ki asked.

"The whore. My whore. Yes. She knew about the robbery. She just didn't realize it. All she had to do was put things together. When I figured that, I knew she had to be silenced, too."

"Did you kill the Wells Fargo detective and the small man in the alley?" Jessie asked.

"Yes, had to do it. You were getting too close."

Maxwell tried to sit up. Ki helped him. Maxwell pointed. "I can see it, a big ball of fire rolling toward me. You've got to stop it. Help me move! No, no. Stop it. Oh, damn, it's too late. Too late!"

Maxwell screamed and fell backward. His cry ended when he hit the sandy soil of the desert. One last gush of air rushed out of his lungs.

Ki shook his head. "He's dead."

Ki went to bring back the packhorse. They checked and found the saddlebags and a gunnysack loaded with gold bricks.

164

There were too many to be all from the Ready Relief. They had found the stolen gold.

Ki lifted Maxwell over the back of the horse, on top of the gold he had worked so hard to steal, and tied him on.

"What about Maxwell's horse?" Ki asked. "It could have gold bars in the saddlebags." They both walked to the edge of the wash and looked at the downed animal. It carried no saddlebags, nowhere that gold could be packed.

Jessie and Ki began the long ride back. They still had most of the day left to make it.

It was a hot ten-mile ride to the top of Banner Grade and on into Julian. They stopped in front of the town marshal's office.

Sheriff Nelson came out and frowned at them.

"Another body, Miss Starbuck?"

"Right, Sheriff. A body, a deathbed confession, and about a hundred thousand dollars worth of gold. Somebody should tell the Wells Fargo man that his stolen gold is safe and sound."

"I'll send somebody. A confession?"

"Yes, Sheriff. Before he died, Washington Maxwell admitted he killed Lawson Blaine, who worked for him. He killed the two men who helped him rob the stage; he killed Sally Wondersome because she knew about the robbery. He also killed the Wells Fargo detective and the small man in the alley. Today he killed one of the men he used to attack the fake gold wagon we sent out."

"Another witness you can talk to is the manager at the Ready Relief mine," Ki said. "He saw Maxwell take the gold from the Ready Relief smeltering shed earlier today and ride toward the desert."

"You kill Maxwell?" Sheriff Nelson asked.

"He died of natural causes, Sheriff," Jessie said. "About two hundred natural rattlesnake bites. He blundered into a rattlesnake sinkhole."

"Oh, damn!" Sheriff Nelson said.

★

Chapter 18

Jessie waved at the sheriff in front of the office. "I'll go see Mr. Laporte and tell him the good news. Ki can give you a report on the three dead men today and Maxwell's deathbed confession."

She left the group of people around the body and walked her horse down to the Wells Fargo office. Q. L. Laporte had just hurried out the front door when she tied up her horse.

"You got him!" Laporte said. "I just heard. News travels fast in Julian. Tell me what happened."

They walked toward the sheriff's temporary office with the town marshal, and Jessie told the Wells Fargo man what happened after they'd parted in the woods.

"We didn't count the gold bricks, but I'll bet they all are there, including some more from the Ready Relief and whatever raw gold Maxwell skimmed off the top. Figured that you'd want to check on it before the sheriff takes a look."

They got there as the undertaker cut Maxwell's body off the horse. The sheriff had started unwrapping the sack of gold when Laporte stepped up.

"I think I better do that, Sheriff. That gold is still in the custody of Wells Fargo. Let's unpack it right now so we have a lot of witnesses as to what's here."

The sheriff nodded, and they laid the bricks of gold out on the boardwalk. They found the original sixteen from the gold wagon robbery, as well as three more bricks marked with the Ready Relief logo and two leather bags filled with smeltered but free-form gold chunks, drips, and globs.

"Sheriff, all I'm concerned about are the sixteen bricks from the robbery. The rest of that gold belongs to the partners in the Ready Relief mine. They should be notified of the theft and the demise of their partner. I think two of them live in San Diego."

Laporte borrowed a wheelbarrow from the hardware store and wheeled the gold bricks down the street to the Wells Fargo office and its big safe. Ki and Jessie walked with him, one in front and one in back. No one made the slightest move to steal the gold.

Laporte put the gold into his safe, and then they walked to the telegraph office. He sent a wire to San Francisco telling the home office that he had recovered the stolen gold and that the man who'd stolen it and shot Detective Irving Davis had confessed and was dead of multiple rattlesnake bites.

On the way back to the Wells Fargo office, Laporte told Jessie and Ki what he'd done after he and Jessie parted.

"All of a sudden the shooting stopped, and I took off for the stage like you said. I figured you two were better at a gun chase than I am. So I cut the two dead horses out of the traces and reharnessed the rig, and we drove it back to town.

"Oh, by the way, that stage is still yours, Miss Starbuck. You bought and paid for it."

Jessie lifted her brows. "I really don't know what to do with it. Why don't you drive it over to the schoolhouse and park it in the playground? It'll be something the children can climb on at recess."

Laporte smiled. "Fine idea. Kids always want to crawl over a stage. I'll get it over there."

They went back to the sheriff's office. Jessie gave the sheriff a statement about the confession and her part in the chase. She signed the paper and realized that the purpose of her trip to Julian was almost over.

"Sheriff, what about the reward? The wanted poster says two thousand dollars dead or alive. I'd like you to put through a wire to the deputy sheriff in Rock Springs, Wyoming, to certify that Maxwell, alias Travis G. Young, has been captured here and is deceased. I want the reward money to go to Agatha Blaine, widow of the man Maxwell killed."

Sheriff Nelson nodded, took down the information, and said he'd get on it before the end of the day.

Jessie and Ki walked toward the hotel.

"We should go tell the widow Blaine about her good fortune," Jessie said. "I just don't want to embarrass her by coming at a bad time."

"A little late in the day for a romp with some lover," Ki said.

Agatha Blaine was properly pleased with the final clearing up about her husband's death.

"The sheriff says he'll apply for the two-thousand-dollar reward for Maxwell and have it sent to you," Ki told her. "It might take a month or so, but you should be getting a check from the bank in Rock Springs."

"Oh, my!" Agatha said. "That's more money than I've ever dreamed of having. What in the world would I do with it?"

"My suggestion would be to put it in a savings account in a San Diego bank, where it will be safe and will bring in a small monthly income from interest." Jessie stood and walked to the door. "We hope the best for you, Agatha," she said.

Outside, they headed for Main Street.

Vince Hirlbach met them. "I hear you did in Maxwell after all. Why didn't you invite me along?"

Jessie grinned. "Because you could have been killed, and then you wouldn't have been able to invite me out to your place for supper."

Vince laughed with delight. "Yes, that's just what I was thinking. So why don't you come to supper?"

Jessie looked at Ki.

"Oh, don't worry about me," he said. "I kind of have an engagement."

"With Happy?" Jessie asked.

"Could be. I have to be inscrutable now." They all laughed.

168

Ki waved and headed for the cafe.

Vince caught Jessie's hand and turned her around, and they walked up the hill toward his house.

"What will the neighbors say about you having a lady guest so late in the day?" Jessie asked him.

"That's not something I'm going to worry about," Vince said. "Anyway I can always say I used to work for you in Wyoming and hope for some more good-paying jobs."

"Yes, you could say that, but nobody would believe you."

"Then I won't tell them. We'll let them guess."

"And gossip?"

"Of course."

His house was as she remembered it, but this time they were in the kitchen, and Vince showed her that he really could cook.

"A bachelor has to do one of two things: learn to cook or go out to eat. I'm turning into a good cook."

"Prove it to me."

He stood there a moment thinking, then snapped his fingers. "I just got some of the latest taste sensation from New York. It's called spaghetti, and might have come from Italy, or China, no one seems to know for sure. It's a pasta with a great sauce over it. First the sauce."

An hour later they ate the spaghetti and a special sauce Vince made from cooked tomatoes and chopped peppers and onions and a whole variety of herbs and spices he mixed in. He made garlic toast and served it with a soft red wine.

After supper Jessie insisted that they do the dishes. She washed.

"Oh, I talked to Sheriff Nelson today before you came back. He's convinced that we need a full-time sheriff's deputy up here. He'll pull some of his budget off and open an office up here with a regular deputy. That means we'll have some real law enforcement in this town."

"Maybe then things will settle down a little," Jessie said.

Vince smiled. "Well, maybe settle down just a little. Things get too calm around here it wouldn't seem like Julian."

Later they sat in front of the fire he had built in the fireplace to take the chill off the October night air.

They were on a robe on the floor watching the wood burn.

"Why can't you stay?" he asked again. "I'd even make an honest woman out of you and not beat you more than necessary. I'd give you at least four small ones that look almost as beautiful as you are, and it would be a good life."

Jessie settled back in his arms and closed her eyes. Some day, she told herself. Some day, but not yet. She turned and kissed him and stared deep into his eyes.

"Vince, it sounds wonderful, but the problem is I'm just not quite ready yet. I have a lot of loose ends to clean up, business things that Daddy started and never got to finish. There are a few people I need to chastise for what they did to him, and a whole city full of people who rely on me and the Starbuck Enterprises. It isn't something I can just walk away from."

"Trapped by your own success?"

"Something like that. More like determined to get things done that need to be done so good people won't be hurt and everyone will benefit. Almost like you doing the best survey you can on a mine and warning which tunnels should be closed down due to extreme gas or structural dangers."

Vince held her gently, kissed the side of her neck, and sighed. "That I can understand. The problem is I can understand all of what you're saying, and I agree with you. You decided when you're heading back?"

"Tomorrow or the next day. I want to be sure everything is settled here first. Also want to be positive that Mr. Laporte gets credit for how he helped us round up Maxwell. We couldn't have done it without his cooperation."

"So we still have tonight," Vince said.

She turned and faced him, kissed his lips gently. "We have all of tonight, and maybe some of tomorrow, who knows? Plans are a little unsure right now."

Vince kissed her soft mouth, and they clung together. The kiss lasted and lasted. Finally she broke away. She reached up and kissed him again, lightly.

"Vincent, it seems like it's getting terribly hot in here. I wonder if you would mind if we took off some of these heavy clothes?"

He smiled. "Not at all, Jessie. In fact I think it's a fine idea. I'll even help you."

Jessie still wore the trousers and shirt she had had on for the long ride. She felt gritty and sweaty and tired, but the sudden glow from Vince's kiss had revived her.

She sat up straight, and his hands came to her neck, opening the high button, then the next four down her chest. As usual she wore nothing under the shirt.

"My god, so beautiful!" Vince said. He had all the buttons open now and pulled the shirt from her pants and spread it aside. "Magnificent, just magnificent." He bent and kissed her breasts softly on the top, then around the sides, and at last he kissed the soft red nipples.

Jessie lifted his face to hers and kissed his lips so lightly that he hardly felt the pressure. He had taken off his jacket when fixing dinner, so now she removed his tie and unfastened the buttons down the front of his shirt.

When he looked at her, Jessie nodded. "Yes, Vince, right here in front of the fire. Right here, right now."

Three long blocks away, in the back two rooms of a rented house, Ki and Happy Tucker lay on her bed, still breathing heavily.

Happy laughed with delight and reached over and kissed Ki's cheek.

"Why is it always better than the last time?" she asked.

"Anticipation," Ki said. "The hoping, the wishing, the wanting, it always makes things more memorable."

"How long can we be memorable?" Happy asked, pushing her short dark hair off her forehead.

"Tonight, some of tomorrow. Not sure. Depends on when Jessie wants to leave."

"We'll make the best of the time we have." She rubbed her hands over his chest. "Where will you go?"

"Home to Texas, west Texas and the Circle Star ranch. Jessie runs a lot of cattle on the home place."

"You're a cowboy, too?"

"When I'm needed. Not my favorite job."

"You just travel around with Miss Jessie, but never sleep with her?"

171

"No. You must understand, she's my master. I am a samurai, a warrior, a protector. Many years ago when she was only a child, her father hired me to be her protector and companion. We could never have any sexual contact. I would lose all of my self-respect and would have to kill myself."

"No!" Happy said. "Don't even think of such a thing. You're far too wonderful to waste."

"Then what can we do about that?"

Happy rolled over on top of him. "See what you can figure out. I have the rest of the night."

Ki and Happy put the time to good use.

The next morning at breakfast Ki found Jessica in her traveling clothes.

"Today?" he asked.

"Yes. There's nothing more for us to do here. The murderer has been caught and has paid the price for his crimes. It's time we get back to the Circle Star. There are so many things that must be done before winter sets in with its full fury. I wonder . . . I wonder how Sun has been doing while we've been gone. He had that sore front leg."

Ki smiled. "Now I know that it's time we were going home. Actually Sun's front leg wasn't all that sore."

"It hurt him," Jessie said. "I hope it's better now." She stared at Ki with a small frown. "Ki, don't waste time over breakfast. We have to catch that seven o'clock stage. Now, hurry your bones. We're going back to the Circle Star . . . and to Sun, the best horse anyone ever had!"

Watch for

LONE STAR AND THE GHOST SHIP PIRATES

130th novel in the exciting LONE STAR
series from Jove

Coming in June!

SPECIAL PREVIEW

At the heart of a great nation lay the proud spirit of the railroads . . .

RAILS WEST!

The magnificent epic series of the brave pioneers who built a railroad, a nation, and a dream.

Here is a special excerpt from book one of this unforgettable saga by Franklin Carter —available from Jove Books . . .

Omaha, Nebraska, Early Spring, 1866

Construction Engineer Glenn Gilchrist stood on the melting surface of the frozen Missouri River with his heart hammering his rib cage. Poised before him on the eastern bank of the river was the last Union Pacific supply train asked to make this dangerous river crossing before the ice broke to flood south. The temperatures had soared as an early chinook had swept across the northern plains and now the river's ice was sweating like a fat man in July. A lake of melted ice was growing deeper by the hour and there was still this last critical supply train to bring across.

"This is madness!" Glenn whispered even as the waiting locomotive puffed and banged with impatience while huge crowds from Omaha and Council Bluffs stomped their slushy shorelines to keep their feet warm. Fresh out of the Harvard School of Engineering, Glenn had measured and remeasured the depth and stress-carrying load of the rapidly melting river yet still could not be certain if it would support the tremendous weight of this last supply train. But Union Pacific's vice president, Thomas Durant, had given the bold order that it was to cross, and there were enough fools to be found willing to man the train and its supply cars, so here Glenn was, standing in the middle of the Missouri and about half sure he was about to enter a watery grave.

Suddenly, the locomotive engineer blasted his steam whistle and leaned out his window. "We got a full head of steam and the temperature is risin', Mr. Gilchrist!"

Glenn did not hear the man because he was imagining what would happen the moment the ice broke through. Good Lord, they could all plunge to the bottom of Big Muddy and be swept along under the ice for hundreds of miles to a frozen death. A vision flashed before Glenn's eyes of an immense ragged hole in the ice fed by two sets of rails feeding into the cold darkness of the Missouri River.

The steam whistle blasted again. Glenn took a deep breath, raised his hand, and then chopped it down as if he were swinging an ax. Cheers erupted from both riverbanks and the locomotive jerked tons of rails, wooden ties, and track-laying hardware into motion.

Glenn swore he could feel the weakening ice heave and buckle the exact instant the Manchester locomotive's thirty tons crunched its terrible weight onto the river's surface. Glenn drew in a sharp breath. His eyes squinted into the blinding glare of ice and water as the railroad tracks swam toward the advancing locomotive through melting water. The sun bathed the rippling surface of the Missouri River in a shimmering brilliance. The engineer began to blast his steam whistle and the crowds roared at each other across the frozen expanse. Glenn finally expelled a deep breath, then started to backpedal as he motioned the locomotive forward into railroading history.

Engineer Bill Donovan was grinning like a fool and kept yanking on the whistle cord, egging on the cheering crowds.

"Slow down!" Glenn shouted at the engineer, barely able to hear his own voice as the steam whistle continued its infernal shriek.

But Donovan wasn't about to slow down. His unholy grin was as hard as the screeching iron horse he rode and Glenn could hear Donovan shouting to his firemen to shovel faster. Donovan was pushing him, driving the locomotive ahead as if he were intent on forcing Glenn aside and charging across the river to the other side.

178

"Slow down!" Glenn shouted, backpedaling furiously.

But Donovan wouldn't pull back on his throttle, which left Glenn with just two poor choices. He could either leap aside and let the supply train rush past, or he could try to swing on board and wrestle its control from Donovan. It might be the only thing that would keep the ice from swallowing them alive.

Glenn chose the latter. He stepped from between the shivering rails, and when Donovan and his damned locomotive charged past drenching him in a bone-chilling sheet of ice water, Glenn lunged for the platform railing between the cab and the coal tender. The locomotive's momentum catapulted him upward to sprawl between the locomotive and tender.

"Dammit!" he shouted, clambering to his feet. "The ice isn't thick enough to take both the weight and a pounding! You were supposed to . . ."

Glenn's words died in his throat an instant later when the ice cracked like rifle fire and thin, ragged schisms fanned out from both sides of the tracks. At the same time, the rails and the ties they rested upon rolled as if supported by the storm-tossed North Atlantic.

"Jesus Christ!" Donovan shouted, his face draining of color and leaving him ashen. "We're going under!"

"Throttle down!" Glenn yelled as he jumped for the brake.

The locomotive's sudden deceleration threw them both hard against the firebox, searing flesh. The fireman's shovel clattered on the deck as his face corroded with terror and the ice splintered outward from them with dark tentacles.

"Steady!" Glenn ordered, grabbing the young man's arm because he was sure the kid was about to jump from the coal tender. "Steady now!"

The next few minutes were an eternity but the ice held as they crossed the center of the Missouri and rolled slowly toward the Nebraska shore.

"Come on!" a man shouted from Omaha. "Come on!"

Other watchers echoed the cry as the spectators began to take heart.

"We're going to make it, sir!" Donovan breathed, banging Glenn on the shoulder. "Mr. Gilchrist, we're by-Gawd goin' to make it!"

179

"Maybe. But if the ice breaks behind us, the supply cars will drag us into the river. If that happens, we jump and take our chances."

"Yes, sir!" the big Irishman shouted, his square jaw bumping rapidly up and down.

Donovan reeked of whiskey and his eyes were bright and glassy. Glenn turned to look at the young fireman. "Mr. Chandlis, have you been drinking too?"

"Not a drop, sir." Young Sean Chandlis pointed to shore and cried, "Look, Mr. Gilchrist, we've made it!"

Glenn felt the locomotive bump onto the tracks resting on the solid Nebraska riverbank. Engineer Donovan blasted his steam whistle and nudged the locomotive's throttle causing the big drivers to spin a little as they surged up the riverbank. Those same sixty-inch driving wheels propelled the supply cars into Omaha where they were enfolded by the jubilant crowd.

The scene was one of pandemonium as Donovan kept yanking on his steam whistle and inciting the crowd. Photographers crowded around the locomotive taking pictures.

"Come on and smile!" Donovan shouted in Glenn's ear. "We're heroes!"

Glenn didn't feel like smiling. His knees wanted to buckle from the sheer relief of having this craziness behind him. He wanted to smash Donovan's grinning face for starting across the river too fast and for drinking on duty. But the photographers kept taking pictures and all that Glenn did was to bat Donovan's hand away from the infernal steam whistle before it drove him mad.

God, the warm, fresh chinook winds felt fine on his cheeks and it was good to be still alive. Glenn waved to the crowd and his eyes lifted back to the river that he knew would soon be breaking up if this warm weather held. He turned back to gaze westward and up to the city of Omaha. Omaha—when he'd arrived last fall, it had still been little more than a tiny riverfront settlement. Today, it could boast a population of more than six thousand, all anxiously waiting to follow the Union Pacific rails west.

"We did it!" Donovan shouted at the crowd as he raised his fists in victory. "We did it!"

Glenn saw a tall beauty with reddish hair pushing forward through the crowd, struggling mightily to reach the supply train. "Who is that?"

Donovan followed his eyes. "Why, that's Mrs. Megan Gallagher. Ain't she and her sister somethin', though!"

Glenn had not even noticed the smaller woman with two freckled children in tow who was also waving to the train and trying to follow her sister to its side. Glenn's brow furrowed. "Are their husbands on this supply train?"

Donovan's wide grin dissolved. "Well, Mr. Gilchrist, I know you told everyone that only single men could take this last one across, but . . ."

Glenn clenched his fists in surprise and anger. "Donovan, don't you understand that the Union Pacific made it clear that there was to be no drinking and no married men on this last run! Dammit, you broke both rules! I've got no choice but to fire all three of you."

"But, sir!"

Glenn felt sick at heart but also betrayed. Bill "Wild Man" Donovan was probably the best engineer on the payroll but he'd proved he was also an irresponsible fool, one who played to the crowd and was more than willing to take chances with other men's lives and the Union Pacific's rolling stock and precious construction supplies.

"I'm sorry, Donovan. Collect your pay from the paymaster before quitting time," Glenn said, swinging down from the cab into the pressing crowd. Standing six feet three inches, Glenn was tall enough to look over the sea of humanity and note that Megan Gallagher and her sister were embracing their triumphant husbands. It made Glenn feel even worse to think that those two men would be without jobs before this day was ended.

Men pounded Glenn on the back in congratulations but he paid them no mind as he pushed through the crowd, moving off toward the levee where these last few vital tons of rails, ties, and other hardware were being stored until the real work of building a railroad finally started.

"Hey!" Donovan shouted, overtaking Glenn and pulling him

181

up short. "You can't fire me! I'm the best damned engineer you've got!"

"*Were* the best," Glenn said, tearing his arm free, "now step aside."

But Donovan didn't budge. The crowd pushed around the two large men, clearly puzzled as to the matter of this dispute in the wake of such a bold and daring success only moments earlier.

"What'd he do wrong?" a man dressed in a tailored suit asked in a belligerent voice. "By God, Bill Donovan brought that train across the river and that makes him a hero in my book!"

This assessment was loudly applauded by others. Glenn could feel resentment building against him as the news of his decision to fire three of the crew swept through the crowd. "This is a company matter. I don't make the rules, I just make sure that they are followed."

Donovan chose to appeal to the crowd. "Now you hear that, folks. Mr. Gilchrist is going to fire three good men without so much as a word of thanks. And that's what the working man gets from this railroad for risking his life!"

"Drop it," Glenn told the big Irishman. "There's nothing left to be gained from this."

"Isn't there?"

"No."

"You're making a mistake," Donovan said, playing to the crowd. The confident Irishman thrust his hand out with a grin. "So why don't we let bygones be bygones and go have a couple of drinks to celebrate? Gallagher and Fox are two of the best men on the payroll. They deserve a second chance. Think about the fact they got wives and children."

Glenn shifted uneasily. "I'll talk to Fox and Gallagher but you were in charge and I hold you responsible."

"Hell, we made it in grand style, didn't we!"

"Barely," Glenn said, "and you needlessly jeopardized the crew and the company's assets, that's why you're still fired."

Donovan flushed with anger. "You're a hard, unforgiving man, Gilchrist."

"And you are a fool when you drink whiskey. Later, I'll hear Fox's and Gallagher's excuses."

"They drew lots for a cash bonus ride across that damned

182

melting river!" Donovan swore, his voice hardening. "Gallagher and Fox needed the money!"

"The Union Pacific didn't offer any bonus! It was your job to ask for volunteers and choose the best to step forward."

Donovan shrugged. He had a lantern jaw, and heavy, fist-scarred brows overhanging a pair of now very angry and bloodshot eyes. "The boys each pitched in a couple dollars into a pot. I'll admit it was my idea. But the winners stood to earn fifty dollars each when we crossed."

"To leave wives and children without support?" Glenn snapped. "That's a damned slim legacy."

"These are damned slim times," Donovan said. "The idea was, if we drowned, the money would be used for the biggest funeral and wake Omaha will ever see. And if we made it . . . well, you saw the crowd."

"Yeah," Glenn said. "If you won, you'd flood the saloons and drink it up so either way all the money would go for whiskey."

"Some to the wives and children," Donovan said quietly.

"Like hell."

Glenn started to turn and leave the man but Donovan's voice stopped him cold. "If you turn away, I'll drop you," the Irishman warned in a soft, all the more threatening voice.

"That would be a real mistake," Glenn said.

Although several inches taller than the engineer, Glenn had no illusions as to matching the Irishman's strength or fighting ability. Donovan was built like a tree stump and was reputed to be one of the most vicious brawlers in Omaha. If Glenn had any advantage, it was that he had been on Harvard's collegiate boxing club and gained some recognition for quickness and a devastating left hook that had surprised and then floored many an opponent.

"Come on, sir," Donovan said with a friendly wink as he reached into his coat pocket and dragged out a pint of whiskey. The engineer uncorked and extended it toward Glenn. "So I got a little carried away out there. No harm, was there?"

"I'm sorry," Glenn said, pivoting around on his heel and starting off toward the levee to oversee the stockpiling and handling of this last vital shipment.

This time when Donovan's powerful fingers dug into

183

Glenn's shoulder to spin him around. Glenn dropped into a slight crouch, whirled, and drove his left hook upward with every ounce of power he could muster. The punch caught Donovan in the gut. The big Irishman's cheeks blew out and his eyes bugged. Glenn pounded him again in the solar plexus and Donovan staggered, his face turning fish-belly white. Glenn rocked back and threw a textbook combination of punches to the bigger man's face that split Donovan's cheek to the bone and dropped him to his knees.

"You'd better finish me!" Donovan gasped. " 'Cause I swear to settle this score!"

Glenn did not take the man's threat lightly. He cocked back his fist but he couldn't deliver the knockout blow, not while the engineer was gasping in agony. "Stay away from me," Glenn warned before he hurried away.

He felt physically and emotionally drained by the perilous river crossing and his fight with Donovan. He had been extremely fortunate to survive both confrontations. It had reinforced the idea in his mind that he was not seasoned enough to be making such critical decisions. It wasn't that he didn't welcome responsibility, for he did. But not so much and not so soon.

The trouble was that the fledgling Union Pacific itself was in over its head. No one knew from one day to the next whether it would still be in operation or who was actually in charge. From inception, Vice President Thomas Durant, a medical doctor turned railroad entrepreneur, was the driving force behind getting the United States Congress to pass two Pacific Railway Acts through Congress. With the Civil War just ending and the nation still numb from the shock of losing President Abraham Lincoln, the long discussed hope of constructing a transcontinental railroad was facing tough sledding. Durant himself was sort of an enigma, a schemer and dreamer whom some claimed was a charlatan while others thought he possessed a brilliant organizational mind.

Glenn didn't know what to think of Durant. It had been through him that he'd landed this job fresh out of engineering school as his reward for being his class valedictorian. So far, Glenn's Omaha experience had been nothing short of chaotic. Lacking sufficient funds and with the mercurial Durant dashing back and forth to Washington, there had been a clear lack of order and leadership. It had been almost three years since Congress had agreed to pay both the Union Pacific and the Central Pacific Railroads the sums of $16,000 per mile for track laid over the plains, $32,000 a mile through the arid wastes of the Great Basin, and a whopping $48,000 per mile for track laid over the Rocky and the Sierra Nevada mountain ranges.

Now, with the approach of spring, the stage had been set to finally begin the transcontinental race. One hundred miles of roadbed had been graded westward from Omaha and almost forty miles of temporary track had been laid. For two years, big paddlewheel steamboats had been carrying mountains of supplies up the Missouri River. There were three entire locomotives still packed in shipping crates resting on the levee while two more stood assembled beside the Union Pacific's massive new brick roundhouse with its ten locomotive repair pits. Dozens of hastily constructed shops and offices surrounded the new freight and switching yards.

There was still more work than men and that was a blessing for veterans in the aftermath of the Civil War joblessness and destruction. Every day, dozens more ex-soldiers and fortune seekers crossed the Missouri River into Omaha and signed on with the Union Pacific Railroad. Half a nation away, the Central Pacific Railroad was already attacking the Sierra Nevada Mountains but Glenn had heard that they were not so fortunate in hiring men because of the stiff competition from the rich gold and silver mines on the Comstock Lode.

Glenn decided he would have a few drinks along with some of the other officers of the railroad, then retire early. He was dog-tired and the strain of these last few days of worrying about the stress-carrying capacity of the melting ice had enervated him to the point of bone weariness.

Glenn realized he would be more than glad when the generals finally arrived to take command of the Union Pacific. He would be even happier when the race west finally began in dead earnest.

185

A special offer for people who enjoy reading the best Westerns published today.

WESTERNS!

NO OBLIGATION

Mail the coupon below

To start your subscription and receive 2 FREE WESTERNS, fill out the coupon below and mail it today. We'll send your first shipment which includes 2 FREE BOOKS as soon as we receive it.